NIGHT SHIFT

NIGHT SHIFT

ISBN: 979-8-83484-595-9

For information contact :
www.ezikembafan.com

Book Layout Design by: Becky Olanrewaju

Photograph by: Nguyen Thanh Ngoc

AN ENTHRALLING STORY THAT WILL LEAVE YOU SPEECHLESS

NIGHT SHIFT

Ezike Mbafan

NOVEL
AUTHOR

DEDICATION

***

This book is dedicated to any body out there that has ever attempted to love. What a feat!

ACKNOWLEDGEMENT

***

Gracie Tsumbu, for peeling me off the floor, seeing the magic in my words and pushing me to write.

My family. For being everything.

Femi Obidare. For editing and polishing my Yoruba.

Becky Olanrewaju and Abiodun Awosokanre.
For showing up at the nick of time and saving the day.
For the Architect, who has put a song in this bird's heart

EXPOSITION

***

I once read a quote about women that both infuriates and fascinates me: "Work like you don't have children and raise children like you don't work."

This mantra embodies the life of the Nigerian woman. No, scratch that, it embodies the life of *every* woman, the impossible standards the vagina is measured by and the blasé born-to-serve-no-questions-asked anthem women live by is even less impressive.

Take me for instance, Abidemi Oluwayemisi Briggs; thirty-one years old, Lagos-born, criminal law attorney at Akin Thomas, Hollaway & Gibson LLP. Dreamer, lover, rebel, wildcard, and hater of fish! Don't ask me why.

My name, Abidemi, tells you half my story. It literally means "born during father's absence". Like, why does the world have to know that? I don't have a clue! So short version: Taiwo Briggs, aka my mother, had me all alone on her kitchen floor while my father,

Adewale Briggs,was away studying in the UK. I am told I came a little earlier than expected. So,before my dad could come home and before my mum could call for help, I popped out - impatient as fuck. Sadly, my mother died some hours later at the hospital from excessive blood loss, but that's a story for another day.

Call me Misi Briggs (Misi is a short form of my second name, Yemisi) "cos I don't have energy to be carrying a whole story for a name around Lagos."Get used to it though, Yoruba is a very curious and interesting ethnicity that marks its children with stories for identity.

I broke things up with my friends-with-benefits, last week. Tolu Makinwa.

Truth is, I'm growing huge feelings for him while he, too self-absorbed to realise it, has been throwing other girls in my face. Like that awful long-breasted girl with the chunky FUPA he was holding hands with at the galleria last Sunday. I mean, I know it's a no-feelings-attached thing between us, but I'm a lady and I'm allowed to change my mind. Besides, his choices in girls are like politically incorrect jokes! Totally cringe worthy. How dare he? The worst part is he didn't even leave her hand when he saw me.And just in case you are wondering about me being part of Tolu's cringe---worthy group of girls, I chose him, not the other way round.

I did it over the phone. The break up. I meant to punish him and I think it worked. I really didn't know it was possible to call somebody fifty times and not get a response and keep going. My pride can't handle that level of rejection. Clearly, Tolu's got none of it.

I miss him though, besides all of this. Guys like Tolu are very rare these days. I'm not even sure if it's Tolu that holds the magic grail of rarity or if he's even capable of it. But the connection between us feels like a volcanic eruption with a life of its own. "Fast lust" is how I like to describe it. I often catch myself calling his name nearly up to ten times in one sentence when we talk. Yeah, that happens when I'm smitten with a man. I can still smell his musk on my sheets - the smell of treachery! - and see his spaced-out teethed smile in my mind's eye. That alarmingly charming smile he exudes when he is content or trying to break my iron clad defences. It's not his musk or alluring smile that make him rare though, any Lagos fraud can give you a smile worthy of your life savings. It's the intravenous chemistry that I haven't felt with anybody else I'm talking about. That type that abruptly quickens the current of my blood whenever he is anywhere around. Trust me, that shit is as rare as alchemy.

Tolu feels like a taboo, exciting, forbidden and adrenaline pumping. Isn't that what it feels like to be alive? Our eyes could communicate virtually every subtle nuance of emotion. I realise now in hindsight what a privilege it is to find that kind of connection with another human and how terribly careless it is to throw it away. His breezy air of quintessential *bad boyness* masks a sensitivity so fragile and an ego so hung up that a phone break-up will literally grind it to goo. I went for the jugular. Go figure!

I'm presently working on a robbery case with a Senior Associate, Oris Ejidawe, the smallest man alive. I mean, he's not a midget or anything like that, although I imagine he must have a pea-sized penis for the depth of pettiness he manages to reach all the time.

Oris Kingsley Ejidawe, or Oke as he is addressed in my office circle behind his back (of course), is the most small-minded human ever to walk this earth. An excellent attorney nonetheless, with a bird's eye view to details, but still too petty. He gives off the kind of energy that makes you want a stiff drink after only being around him for five minutes. A heavyset man with glasses thick as a slice of wonder bread, it's an open secret in the office that his wife left him for her lover and took their only son with her. I can't say I blame her much! Needless to say, I can't wait to conclude this case and escape from this toxic energy. This is my year of self-care and Oke is too small (literally) to derail me.

It was a humid Monday morning in April at the Ikeja High Court when the Registrar informed us that our case had been adjourned till the subsequent month. We had hoped for judgment that day and we were anticipating an acquittal for the accused person, Judith Balogun, who allegedly stabbed her boyfriend while being married to Elder Segun Balogun who has now filed for a divorce. The acquittal would mean everything to her. But alas, another adjournment. Moreover, I would have been done with Mr. Petty over here at least for this month. He was having a go at the

Registrar over the impromptu adjournment and his voice could be heard all over Ikeja. I decided to wait in the car. It was the last day of my three-day juice cleanse; I was battling a banging headache from all the starvation and had no physical energy for drama. I really hoped we'd leave the main land on time that day, judgment or adjournment. I had a date with the girls that evening, plus I would finally be eating actual food for the first time in three days. Naturally, I was in no mood for Lagos traffic or Mr. Oke.

CHAPTER TWO

CLAN

***

So me and the girls are checking out Warehouse, a new spot off Abimbola Cole Road in Lekki. As always, Gogo was the first to get there and she's been shouting over the phone since, demanding that I showed up. Mtcheeew! A girl can't even be fashionably late in peace again!

Let me introduce my girls by the way, you already know early bird Gogo. Full name: Ngozi Mbagwu. We met at Lagos Law school and ended up sharing a flat close to Ozumba Mbadiwe road. Gogo is super fascinating, at least to me she is, because my first impression of her turned out to be the complete 360 degrees opposite of who she really is. She looks everything like the spoilt brat, *ajẹbota* type girl and why not? Apart from being the only daughter of Major General Clifford Mbagwu, she graduated summa cum laude from the University of Warwick, England, speaks four languages fluently - Igbo, Yoruba, French and English- and has lived on four continents. Oh, I forgot; she's the best cook you'll ever read about.

There is however a toughness about Gogo that doesn't quite suit the first impression she exudes. Talk about growing up military.

Then there is Coventry-schooled Lola. Pronounced 'low-la' as she demands to be called. Full name: Oluwalolami Kikelomo Pitan. Gogo and I met Lola years ago at a Guaranty Trust Bank Lagos fashion week when she was nursing ideas of breaking into the fashion world. Our connection was instant. We bonded over three things: 1) we absolutely, collectively as a nation bound with freedom, peace and unity, do not deserve Burna Boy. 2) A cerebral, nice smelling weirdo guy any day over crotch-clenching, minch-hunting Lagos guys and 3) Maki Oh, Gozelgreen, Mai Atafo and Bridget Awosika are Nigeria's best exports to the world. Lola is skinny from years of her dedication to Karl Lagerfeld's diet, not as tall as she looks. Intense, with a permanent resting bitch face. She always says a girl can never be too rich or too thin. She is one of those girls you meet who exude high nosed unreachability and she's unapologetic about every single second of her uppity life. It's all a mask though; she's one of the nicest and goofiest people I know, but she reserves that side of herself for behind closed doors.

So that's my circle.

Gogo works at Schlumberger Nigeria while Lola is a self-employed stylist and content creator. She recently resigned from the World Health Organisation to pursue her life-long passion of creating and becoming her brand, POK,pronounced "poke".Everything that she knows about style and fashion, she has interpreted into that brand and it's turned out wonderfully.

I always imagined it POK stood for her initials backwards but she insists to this day that it's an acronym for

Perfect.Original.Kickass. To Lola's credit though, her work is steadily gaining clout. POK is edgy, fresh, versatile and fluid. This brand caters to a wide range of styles; the simple, the classy, the edgy, the androgynous. Recently, she created a few subs under her brand, which to me is genius. POK Basics, POK Festives, POK Streetstyle, POK Classics and POK Essentials for him and for her. POK Essentials which by the way, is my favorite sub focuses on 'must-haves' for men and women. Like a white shirt. I think her white shirts are remarkable by the way; I'd wear the male and female ones any day. Lola recently styled Tiwa Savage for her latest music video and Chimamanda Ngozi Adichie for a paper presentation in Brussels.

Warehouse turned out to be exquisite and very literal I must say! with piped ceiling, tasteful furnishing and the creative use of different seat styles; tyre seats, wooden seats, seats carved out of tree trunks and barrels, all arranged carelessly you'd think, but with evident deliberateness. "I love it!" Plus they sold everything! traditional and continental cuisine, boli and roasted fish, suya, asun, beer, spirits, name it. It was hard not to imagine that the owner must have thought of WAREHOUSE in every sense of the word down to the menu. And the food portions?, Impressive.

Lola had Greek salad, which she picked at all through the evening. I had *boli* and peppered chicken, after which I nursed a black Russian, a not-so-simple mix of Vodka Absolut 100 and coffee liqueur. " The good Lord knows I didn't do juice cleanse and drive through Ikeja traffic to come and be chewing on vegetables like a goat." Gogo ordered for fries and peppered chicken. The gist of the evening was: the magical powers of Edy's vagina.

Edy is a mutual friend of ours,more like a spare wheel to our clan of three. Full name: Edima Okon. She shows up sparingly and serves up juicy stories like die! Edy knows all the people that matter on the Lagos scene and sometimes gets us VIP passes to the most lavish parties around Eko. You never know with her though; she's very stealth in a trompe l'oeil way and gives a whole new meaning to the phrase, "The more you look, the less you see."

The word about town is that Edy is now dating three men simultaneously, among which are two married Lagos 'big boys' who have literally 'jammed' themselves at her place severally, but none has refused to back down. The plot thickens...... none of these guys seem upset with her for the multiple dating, instead, they are at loggerheads, competing over who will win her affections (serious kayanmata alert). One of the contenders, Otunba Ajani, is threathening to buy her a house on Banana Island. The third man lives in Abuja, an older man with I-don't-give-a-fuck money, who enjoys having Edy, his fantasy woman, at his beck and call. Abuja Daddy has been paying the rent of her lavish three bedroom apartment at Lekki Phase 1 for years. The dilemma now is that Edy is working overtime to keep all "three wise men" happy and contented. According to her, the older man, Abuja Daddy, is her sponsor, Ajani on the other hand gives her tsunamic orgasms, while the third wise man is the love of her life.

"That explains the almost miserable look she was wearing the other day I ran into her at the mall." I told the girls. "Yeah,'cos we now know the size of her grind." Gogo added, a little nonchalantly. We all laughed out. "That grind ehn, e go pain!" Lola said in one of her extremely rare pidgin moments. Edy was one of those girls you could hardly put a finger on what they actually did for a living or how they made money to fund their lavish lifestyle. Gogo said that she was a Personal Assistant to a former Ogun State's First Lady. Lola said she thought Edy presently worked at NNPC Abuja, where she did three days at work and was back to Lagos by Thursday. But I remember Edy telling me when we first met that she was a Special Assistant to the then Ogun State Governor. In any case, we still didn't know what she did for a living and quite frankly, we no longer cared.

While Lola was wondering-out-loud how she could get her hands on Edy's kayanmata contact, Gogo was acting very distracted. At this point, she couldn't take it anymore and she planted her left hand in our faces and there it was! A clean-cut diamond, huge enough to put out our eyes. She was a little upset we hadn't noticed the rock sooner, almost weighing down her middle finger. Who could blame us? When Edy's movie-worthy life keeps throwing us off balance like ludo dices. "Awww. It's beautiful!" Lola and I chorused like giddy school girls. Gogo passed her well-manicured hand round the table for closer inspection. I hate it though, not the diamond of course, it's perfect. I hate the idea of Gogo marrying Molade and I can't say I didn't see it coming to this. I think she is making a mistake and I had dreaded this day for months. She, announcing her engagement to us and we faking happiness; Lola and I have talked about this privately and agreed that we both hated the idea. Lola doesn't feel as strongly about it as I do though. According to her, Gogo is grown and knows what she wants. But we decided that I should find the appropriate words to express our reservations about the relationship, because as far as friendship dynamics go, Gogo and I are kinda, sorta two-peas-in-the-pod closer to each other than we are with Lola. Maybe it's because we live together. I mean, don't get me wrong, Molade Okoya is a decent guy and he comes from long money. Gogo is high maintenance and he matches her material and maybe even sexual needs, but I don't think he measures up to her emotional needs. It's just, I don't think he 'gets' her and she's just settling for an idea of who she thinks she should be with. He's not asking her to change or anything like that but she's just not herself when she's around him. It always seems like she's about to say something then she'll pause and say something else. Like she's searching for the words that will make her who she needs to be for the relationship to work. It's exhausting to watch.

Let me explain further.

Gogo speaks good French. She and I goof around all the time and break out sporadically in French at the market in our side-talks over prices, or when we assess a guy either of us just met, right in his face and he has no clue, which to me is always the best part. One time at church, this guy walked up to me and started making small talk, which I absolutely hate by the way. I quickly found Gogo and introduced them just so I could shut him up. He was looking at her like how a starving lion would look at an unsuspecting antelope. "Je pense qu'il est stupide", said Gogo. "Je sais mais il est tellement mignon." I replied. At a loss, the clueless 'starving-lion' was like, "Wait, are you guys not Nigerians?" Oh!, we love messing with them like that. Lola isn't spared either. Sometimes just to get under her skin, Gogo and I will go on a long French banter. This irritates her so much because, she speaks only English and Yoruba. She however, chooses to speak only the former (I think this is a good place to add that if you ever speak to Lola in Yoruba, she'll reply in English).

I started speaking French from an early age, growing up with Aunt Kehinde, my mother's twin, whom I fondly call Mummy Kay and her then French partner, Timothée Moreau. Mummy Kay practically became more French than her lover, Uncle Mo (as she insisted I addressed him). Yesso! That's the level the love was shaking her. So all we spoke at home was French.

Gogo, Lola and I also bonded over an overdose of swear words in our conversations and I imagined that our life partners, or husbands, or whatever, would know this about us. However, none of these fun facts or traits surface whenever Gogo is around Molade. No French, no cusses, nothing. Even when I say something to her in French as a side talk when he is around, she responds in English. Of course, I suppose it is for Molade's benefit, since he neither speaks nor understands the language. She has also never cussed in his presence and I just feel like that exciting goofy core of her disappears whenever he shows up. She thinks Molade is the bees' knees, so we all just act like straight arrows whenever he is around.

I brought it up the other night when we were both drunk and she shut it down so fast, I almost felt like she was evading hearing the truth. Since then, she avoids talking all things Molade Okoya with me, only Lola gets that privilege. I know that real friends are expected to reinforce one another's sense of self, rather than try to change one another. I mean, maybe I even overstepped my bounds a little bit. I've asked myself if I'm jealous, or I'm simply trying to bring us back to the place we once were: two roommates, watching movies, exploring Lagos, judging everybody, being classy and hood, all in one breath, in a way only a Lagos girl knows how to. I think my only concern is her happiness though. But I totally get it. Gogo is just like most women when they meet someone they really like; they tend to hide themselves and try to morph into whoever the new man needs them to be so that the relationship can last. God knows I've morphed a few times in the past. The problem is, it only takes a little while for most girls to realize that we can't stay contoured forever. Sooner than later, we need to straighten up and stretch out. And, straighten up and stretch out we all do. Eventually.

CHAPTER THREE
BACK STORY

***

*I*t was in the wee hours of a Tuesday, 30th January that I popped out and my mum lost her life. It has felt like an unnecessary exchange to me for the most of mine.

Taiwo Ajayi Briggs, commonly known to her friends as Tai, was five feet nine, full head of hair and clear brown skin the color of Joke Silva's. The only picture of her I have is one in which she's wearing a dark colored mini skirt, an off-white blouse with oversized sleeves and a chic Afro. With her long endless legs tucked at the feet into a pair of triangular heeled Mary-Janes and crossed at the ankles, she is leaning against a red first generation 1974 Buick Regal sedan with a playful, almost flirty smile on her face. Mummy Kay says they were 20 years old when that picture was taken and their father,Otunba Ajayi or Baba Agba, as he is commonly called had just officially allowed mum drive the sedan. Mum had however been driving it unofficially behind Baba Agba's back and perfecting her driving skills.

Tai and Kay, as they were so famously called, seemed to be the coolest duo in Ikeja GRA back then I heard. Their mother ,Eniola Ibiwunmi Ajayi,was eight months pregnant when she died in a car accident just about the time the twins turned eleven. Baba Agba went on to marry two other wives who gave him about a dozen children between them, but he never really got over the loss of Eniola, his first wife and first love.

Mummy Kay describes her twin as tongue-in-cheek, spirited and passionate. She was quick to laugh and even quicker to love, but she was the most vindictive human that ever breathed. She loved as hard and as easily as she could hate. Mummy Kay says that when they were in Queens College, Tai once caught her beloved boyfriend cheating on her. What did she do? She marched straight to the boy's house on the next street in their estate (I think Mummy said his name was Daniel or so)and in a very theatrical fashion told his parents on her knees, with a soulful, quiet but scornful cry, that while she had made a dreadful mistake and explored her sexuality too soon with their son Daniel, he had in turn given her an STI. She lamented that Daniel was her first and that she had apologized to her own parents earlier and was not even sure if they would ever forgive her. Mummy Kay said she was shocked at the mastery of how easily Tai lied and could work up a convincing cry. It was nothing short of a miracle how her split personality act always got them out of trouble and Tai did get into a lot of trouble back then. She knew that her twin was a virgin up until they got into University. The 'explored-her-sexuality' line became a private joke between them.

Needless to say, nobody cared for Daniel's version of the story;

his parents even felt sympathy for Tai and offered to take her to the hospital, but she told them that disappointed as she was, her mum had already taken her and she was well on her medication. Poor Daniel was grounded for all of his teenage life. Mummy Kay says the news was all over their estate and shortly afterwards, Daniel was sent to school abroad and they never saw him again.

Daddy says his wife's energy was fierce and risky in a way that seemed like she could cut you(and I totally believe him) and yet she was loving and soft at the same time. There were no halves and halves with Taiwo Briggs and no grey areas either; Daddy says it was either black or white and no space for in-betweens with her. She seemed to me like someone who when you were with, you knew you were into something solid; kind of like the female version of the character Okonkwo in Things fall apart. I wish I were like that sometimes. Very definite in my choices and all round badass.

Mummy Kay says they were born only about one minute apart, but my mother carried on like she was older than her by two and a half millennia. Interestingly, everybody else treated her likewise, like the older and first born of Baba Agba. I wonder what kind of mum she would have been or if we would have gotten along. She sounds nothing like me really.

After her death, Daddy was shattered and Mummy Kay offered to raise me. That way, Daddy, who had only been married to my mum for barely 8 months, could focus on picking himself up and maybe even get married again (the sheer convenience of male privilege!).

I grew up in Camden town, Northwest London. My first home, two weeks old from Lagos, Nigeria, was a small low-cost flat in Arlington House. Mummy Kay was in Nursing School at that time. Later, we moved to Gloucester Crescent when French man Timothée 'Yang' Moreau first locked eyes with my aunt in the hospital ward and proceeded to bourrée into her life.

As far as I am concerned, up until I was twenty years old, Timothée, or Uncle Mo as I called him then, was the perfect fit with my Mummy Kay. Their friends had nicknamed him Yang from a private joke that he was the Yang to mummy Keyinde's 'Yin' and the name stuck. He was like a breath of fresh air after a string of very awful relationships my aunt had endured. I loved their love. They never officially married, but were partners and a team at home, alternating who cooked, who cleaned and who watched me after school, depending on their schedules. It was a good time to be alive for a little lost girl like me. Before he came into our lives, Mummy Kay raised me on Yoruba language; she often said that the Oyinbos will teach me English at school. But when Uncle Mo joined our duo, French became our official language. From then, Mummy Kay and I only spoke Yoruba when Daddy visited and on the rare occasions when Uncle Mo was not around. Mummy Kay said it was a good opportunity for both of us to learn the language but I knew it was more than that. Who would blame her? Women have been known from the beginning of history to exchange their ikigai, their identities, their personal passions and values for a man's comfort and acceptability. It's like how a woman who marries into another tribe in Nigeria is told she is not serious about the marriage when she hasn't learnt to speak her husband's language. Or how in most African cultures, she is regarded as inadequate if she hasn't given birth to a male child. So, we spoke English and French at first when Uncle Mo moved in with us and as Mummy Kay and I got the hang of French, it became our official language around the house.

Daddy would drop by our little flat to visit on holidays for a few hours, then disappear for months. Those holidays were special times I loved and hated with equal intensity. I loved that Mummy Kay made all things Nigerian on those special days. Amala and ewedu, Gbegiri, Ewaagoyin, Eforiro, Iresi, Eyin, Dodo, Asun and igbin. It was always such an extravagant buffet. We would have a few other Nigerian friends over, mostly Daddy and his friends and a few others from Mummy Kay's work place. However, I hated that my Nigerian food experience was somehow tied to my father.

Mummy Kay and Uncle Yang did their best for me, I can't lie. But I always felt like something was missing. The feeling of inadequacy followed me around like a shadow and as I grew older, I had this deep-seated hunch, premonition or whatever, that my Dad resented me or secretly blamed me for my mum's death. It wasn't anything he did or said; I guess it was in what he didn't do or say. Like why couldn't I go visit him on holidays? Why was he the only one visiting? And why didn't he ever take me out anywhere? When he eventually got married and moved to Nigeria, why did he abandon me? Why couldn't I move back with him and his new wife? He just started his life all over again with a brand new family like mum and I never existed. In my early teenage years, I started dodging those dreaded visits of his when we hardly had anything to say to each other and he'd spend the hour talking more to my aunt about Lagos and all things Nigeria, while they made me sit around there pretending that he was visiting me. I hated it.

My life outside the house at the time was equally treacherous. I was a luke warm student at school and emotionally inaccessible. In some way, I think I stayed that way. I am poor when it comes to parents; from a dead mother at birth and an absentee surviving father who didn't have any use for his own child. So I sought comfort in older men. For most of my teenage life I think I was controlled by what Sigmund Freud calls the ID part of the mind. You know, that part of the mind that holds all of humankind's most basic and primal instincts. My mind was impulsive and unconscious and it desired to seek immediate satisfaction. It was like I didn't have a grasp on any form of reality or consequence when it came to dating older men. For instance, my first, Andrew Caste from Manchester.

I'll never forget Andrew. Boyish, looking not a day over twenty, with grey eyes and hair always neatly cut like he was drafted for the army. He was 33 years old while I was 15. I know! The cradle-snatching situation of it all. Right? But to my young mind, it was a beautiful liaison and you must know, I have always been the girl with strong opinions. I needed a break from myself, from my father's dreaded visits, from Timothée (with the bloody accent somewhere on the 'e'), from Mummy Kay's ignorance, all of it! I was unraveling and it was a good time to have met Andrew Caste. It was a Thursday afternoon and I was rushing through my essay which I turned in late by the way. Seated by one of the gigantic windows at Café Lite, one of my favorite spots in London, he came in to grab a latte. My back was turned to the front door, with furrowed brows and a bent back, full-bars concentration, tapping frantically at my computer keys and this dude walks over to me and says, "I saw that you and I chose the same scarf today so I came over to say hello". He had wrapped around his neck the same Gucci scarf, same color as I had around mine. Baba Agba bought me the scarf as a present for my fifteenth birthday when he visited the UK. He always said I was a sophisticated girl just like my mum and he delighted in buying me expensive gifts. Personally though, I just thought he felt sorry for me growing up with my aunt and no father or mother around. So as I was trying to find the right words to say to this random stranger that apparently wanted us to bond over our matching scarves, he smiled and said "I'm Andrew by the way. Andrew Caste." Hand extended out for a handshake. I took it and mumbled "Misi. Misi Briggs". He said "See you around Misi Briggs." and he was gone. I sat still for a while pondering the randomness of this meeting and I was quite certain of one fact, this stranger was not a Londoner. The locals were almost repulsed by friendliness, especially from strangers. Quite frankly, on any other day, I probably would have found that kind of directness from a random stranger rude, but not today. There was something rather endearing about him. He was now at my window outside, he made a face and left. From that moment, I was taken. What refreshing spontaneity in the middle of drab, old, mind-your-own-nose London. Later, we would joke that his randomness was a fundamental British problem that needed to be tackled debate-style at the House of Commons!

I went back to Café Lite everyday afterwards, hoping he'll come back for another latte. One rainy morning, he did. I swear, I held back from giving that grown man a full-on hug. We talked for what seemed like forever and exchanged numbers. Andrew gave the greatest conversations, full stop. The kind that makes a girl come away feeling like she was the best-laid plan. How do I explain this? It wasn't like he was sitting around making small talk or dirty nasty talk; he could be talking about parliament or World War 2 and I'd still hand him my panties. He was both cerebral and virile, very rare you see. I told him I was fifteen at the time and he acted like our friendship was nothing sexual. Indeed it wasn't, at first. And I got really comfortable and could tell him anything. I would call him up at odd hours to talk and he listened. I couldn't wait to kiss him. One day at his place, I went for it and he didn't stop me. That made me feel so powerful, you know, how a grown man makes a little girl feel like she's calling the shots when in actual fact, he was. It was an affair because of my age and no one had to know. I think the "tabooey" nature of things made it even more exciting for me, until he told me he was getting married to Alison, the school teacher from Kent. I mean, I would've gladly shared him with her if he liked. But he was paranoid that Alison would find out about my age, our affair and everything. Things ended as abruptly as they had started. Even though I grieved privately, I never went back or spared him a thought. I was so psychologically removed I could have cared less or so, I thought. If I could describe my life back then in a phrase, it'll be "Live as well as you dare!" And dared I did.

After Andrew, I rebounded with a boy at school who fancied me. I was older than him by a year or two. Can't remember his name now, Jonathan or Jonah something. He was so clingy and was always about the emotions it reminded me of why I preferred older men. Older men are like business partners. You can rely on them to bail you out when you are in serious trouble because they need you to come to the 'business' light, happy, spontaneous and maybe a little crazy. I learnt early in life that older men don't need your emotions all over the place because they deal with all of that in their personal lives with spouses or family and this suited me perfectly. I wasn't looking for any heavy stuff, so these old crows were perfect for me. My time with them taught me sarcasm and a razor-sharp wit. I had my first beer and my first spliff with these grown men. What's not to like? Besides, there was nothing more thrilling than being the object of their passions. It was like being the heroine of my own private film. I established early in my life my eternal love for men. But for women? I have a very low opinion of women. They always manage to make me nervous. I'm not sure if it's my early life experience of a dead mum or the fact that my Aunty Kay was so ignorant when her lover molested me all that time. Women just have a way of sapping my self-confidence. I mean, one would think that with an absentee father like mine, I would have a lower opinion of men, but no! For me, men are solid and safe and the older they are, the better. I remember forty-year old widower Kwame Smith who wore a sluggish inferiority of an older man courting a younger woman. Well in my case, a girl. Frugal ol' Kwame, British-Ghanaian born. I rolled my first joint under the careful tutelage of Kwame in his cozy flat in East village, Stratford. I remember he took the joint from me, took a hard drag and then proceeded to blow me a slow shotgun, that's blowing the smoke right into my mouth from his. It was all so sensual and dangerous and I always came away with a little sunlight between me and my problems. If only Mummy Kay knew half the things I got up to those days! I loved going to Kwame's flat because he made the best *banku* and tilapia in all of London. He also taught me how to make *waakye*, a very tasty Ghanaian meal made with rice. I still remember Kwame fondly; his signature mix of acid critique and avuncular reassurance always left me with conflicting feelings of a blessing and a curse. I could run down the list of my sordid older men affairs/rebounds but that'll bore you. So I'll tell you about Timothée and how I came back to Nigeria.

Like you already know, Timothée, or Uncle Mo, was home with my Mummy Keyinde, playing the quintessential partner. He is the only 'father figure' I had growing up. By the time I turned fifteen, Daddy had remarried and was moving back to Nigeria without me. A year before that, my world crashed. My idea of love and everything I knew fell apart all because my dear Uncle Mo (I stopped calling him that afterwards and quite frankly, the man has so many names he should have just been a Yoruba man! Sighs) thought I was old enough to become his 'play thing'. How do you watch a child grow up and then turn around and want to sleep with her? It was all so sinister, like a witch's brew. He would come into my room on nights when Mummy Kay was night shifting at the hospital and fondle me. I remember him saying it was just 'play' between me and him and no one had to know. I'm not even sure when exactly it started. But I remember vividly one day after a bed time banter which he and I usually had about life, the weather, music, you know, anything. I had been experiencing a sharp pain in my neck for about two days and he offered to massage it. His hands didn't stay on my neck or shoulders for very long however. They roamed around all the way to my chest, kneading and squeezing with an unexpected speed while it seemed like his breathing was accelerating audibly. I remember freezing in shock, but mostly in confusion. Then my reflexes kicked in and I smacked his hands off me and ran to the door. He apologized and acted like it was an innocent mistake but his eyes said differently. Those shifty beady eyes, I should've known this was just a start to something dark and forbidden. How was I going to tell Mummy Kay this? And should I even tell her and destroy her perfect little world with her 'perfect' little Timothée Moreau? I have often wondered to this day why it is that I am so careful with other people's secrets? How and why did Timothée know that I was the type of person to keep quiet and pretend to be a stranger before his secret? Is there a prototype for the type of person that can be molested and keep quiet about it?

The next time, he seemed a little bolder, like he had broken the ice with the first 'almost-attempt' and now I was supposed to be more willing. I was napping in my room that morning after a long night with my study group. It was a short Easter break and schools were resuming the week after. Silly me, I hadn't made anything of his first attempt, so I hadn't thought to lock my bedroom door. I even doubted myself a little and thought maybe it was really a mistake like he had claimed. I woke up with a start when I felt his hand up my thighs, under my sleeping robe. I ran to a corner and threatened to tell my aunt. He got up from my bed, faced me squarely and said, "That's a tough line to walk, Demi." He was the only one that called me Demi and I have hated that name ever since.

"It's your word against mine, mon amour, and do you really think Kay will believe you?" Timothée was the worst kind of vile creature, but he wasn't stupid. He knew his sterling record with Mummy Kay would speak for him. What more, for years he had tried to have a baby with my aunt and when that wasn't looking feasible, he suggested they legally adopt me as theirs. At the time, I thought it was a brilliant idea but Daddy wouldn't hear of it. I hated him a little deeper for refusing the Frenchman and my aunt's request. He didn't want me and he wouldn't let anybody else have me and to my young mind, Adewale Briggs was a wicked man, end of story. "Don't call me that, putain de bâtard." I yelled back at him. I followed his eyes and they were perversely rested on my scantily dressed body. Just then, he smiled at me with something that I recognized as longing. It was the most sinister look I'd ever seen. I ran downstairs into the guest bathroom and locked the door. I sat there on the cold floor for about an hour before I heard him leave the house. I emerged slowly and noiselessly from the bathroom and tip toed around the house to make sure he was really gone, then I locked the front and back doors. Even though he had both keys, I figured I would hear him turning his key and that was enough time for me to hide before he got in. I called Mummy Kay "Màámi, a nílátis'ọ̀rọ̀. We need to talk." I said, trying my best to still my voice and not cry. She heard the anxiety in my voice anyway and yelled into the phone "Yemisi, kíló n ṣẹlẹ?" I was quiet and I could tell she was getting worried. "Kíni ọ̀rọ̀ náà?" She sounded desperate. I hung up before I could break down into an endless ugly cry. Trust me to be so "in control" even in a near rape situation. I hated crying. I think I still do. I hate the desperation that comes with that verb and everything it connotes. I hate the hopelessness of it, I hate the vulnerability of it, the relinquishing of control of my emotions even if it's just for a short time and most of all, this is no joke ladies and gentlemen, I hate the ugly faces I make (and can't help making) when I cry. I am your quintessential ugly-cry girl. The first time Tolu Makinwa saw me cry, he later joked about it that he thought I was smelling something extremely repulsive! My facial muscles slowly start to pull away from my face and my lips start to stretch like I'm about to break out into the biggest smile you have ever seen. Just then, the T between my eyes creases up so hard my nostrils have no choice but to rumple up, way up, disfiguring any form of beauty my face once held. Yeah, my cry face is that bad. I loved Tolu a little more for the audacity to tell me what I know no one around me had the guts to say to my face. In my mind, crying feels like handing over control to who or whatever hurt me. Little wonder though, because I am told I didn't cry at birth. Taiwo Briggs thought I was still birth. When her neighbor, Mrs Oko, who is also a midwife came into the kitchen-turned-delivery room, she found a screaming Taiwo and a quiet baby on the floor and proceeded to check if I was breathing at all. Turned out I was. I am told she proceeded to dangle me by the foot and smack me; only then did I start to cry and only then did Taiwo stop to scream. So, I think that was when my no-woman-no-cry mode was activated because when Adewale Briggs left London for Nigeria to start his new life without me but with his new wife, I did not cry. I refused to waste my tears on an undeserving sperm donor. I did not cry when Andrew Caste abruptly ended our inappropriate love affair. I refused to cry when (long before Timothée 'Yang' Moreau showed up in our lives) Adewale Briggs, aka my daddy, didn't show up at a class project that required fathers to come and talk to the class about why they loved being fathers and I was the only kid who didn't present that day because as I later found out, Daddy forgot and got the dates mixed up. And there it is, my non-crying chart.

Mummy Kay met up with me at Café Lite. I could see she was visibly panicked and I wished things were different. I wished her Moreau knight was genuinely knightly and shiny. "I have talked to Baba Agba and I'm getting enrolled into an all-girls' boarding school." I blotted out the minute she sat down. I had a bad habit of talking to my grandfather first about things that bothered me before my aunt even heard about them, especially when those concerns involved money. Mummy Kay and I were comfortable in London because she worked extra hard for our lives. I dreaded burdening her with any extra bills, not that she ever minded though. She hated hearing about my concerns from her father, it infuriated her. She'd always hoped that we would have a tighter, closer bond like a mother and a daughter, but I was a troubled child who could never seem to shake off the feeling that I wasn't enough. Baba Agba was always my way out, especially when I was "up to no good". He never really got over my mother's death, who was rumored to be his favorite child and I guess spoiling me was his lifelong resolve. Besides, I'd watched Mummy Kay work so hard for the life she was building for us and I didn't want to be the party pooper. I had planned to tell her Timothée had a "hot pack", that he was all too willing to share with me, but when she sat down in that café, looking so worried and stressed from all the endless shifts at the hospital, I immediately felt sorry for her. She had never really been lucky in love, but then again, which Briggs/Ajayi women were? I decided spur of the moment to put out the boarding house story to Mummy Kay early enough as her wrath was a whole other schmaltz and could take weeks to ease off, then later convince Baba Agba about actually paying my fees and all. "Kíl'eléyìí Yemisi?" She said, desperate. "What is this all about? Is this all I get after everything we've been through? Ọmọ aláìmoore. Why on earth would you have a conversation with Baba Abga about boarding school and just inform me in a coffee shop Yemisi? You ungrateful child! Talk now? Kíni gbogbo èyí?" She always spoke Yoruba and interpreted in English whenever she was anxious, afraid or angry. This was a case of all three. "Wait, Yemisi. Ṣ'émil'ọmọẹ? Am I your child? That you would call me out here to direct me on where you want to go and not go?" People were beginning to notice the oncoming tiff at our table. "Mummy Kay, he is touching me inappropriately!" I shouted. I shocked myself. I was supposed to sit quietly through her verbal wrath and wait for her to storm out in annoyance at my silence, then call Baba Agba immediately. That was my grand plan, but something changed when she was hurling Yoruba-interpreted-in-English at me. I am extraordinarily patient, provided I get my way in the end, but this wasn't going my way at all. It felt like I was the one at fault for Timothée's bad behavior and that made me angry. Why should I shield that fool and take the heat? I was ready for the consequences if Mummy Kay did not believe me. I was fed up to the back teeth with everything and everyone anyway. I was fed up with "pervy"Timothée, I was angry with Mummy Kay for not noticing that something was wrong, that I had to tell her about it myself, I was especially fed up with the

35

possibility that she might not believe me and I would have to prove myself and maybe my innocence as well to her. "Ehn! Kí lo so? What did you just say Yemisi?" This was the part I hated the most and was trying to avoid. "I said your boyfriend has been trying to get his hands on me since and I just want to leave the house so he can stop. I was not entirely sure if you'd believe me, that's why I thought I should go away to boarding house and save you all the trouble. Gbogboẹ̀n'ìyẹn."

Her look changed instantaneously from werewolf to something in between physical pain and delirious anxiety. She rested her back against the sit and became very still. In all my time living with Keyinde Ajayi, I have seen her red-eye-furious only once, when I was six years old and a white boy in my class called me bootlip. Mummy Kay stormed over to my school in her nurse scrubs during her lunch break the next day and gave the principal her red-eyed-voice-lowered-to-a-pitch piece of mind. This was the second time I was seeing her that furious. Other times when she's just upset, she's dramatic and almost theatrical, going on and on about it in her characteristic Yoruba-interpreted-to-English which could last the whole week. When she is furious however, she becomes still, red-eyed (literally) and her voice is barely heard. Her tone will become so low and elocution-class that you heard her with your bones and not your ears. I was making to go get us two coffees and with some luck, distance myself physically from her imminent volcanic rage. I knew she was blaming me for it all and quite frankly I needed time to ready myself when she said in her stillness, "Oluwayemisi Abidemi Briggs, sit down and tell me every single detail I need to know about what that bastard has been doing." When I heard the word "bastard", the relief I felt was incomparable. I broke down then and cried the tears I had been refusing to let out for most of my teenage/young adult life. I couldn't stop crying and Mummy Kay didn't try to stop me. She believed me and didn't blame me for it! My biggest fears didn't come true. Gosh! If I knew differently, I would have told her from the first day Timothée looked at me weird. She just held me, still, red-eyed, smoldering from what she just heard, but loving in comfort. Right there in that small café, my aunt and I cultivated a whole new bone-deep bond, the type she had been wanting us to have. And oh, I forgot to mention, she and I switched back to speaking Yoruba again and that has never changed.

CHAPTER FOUR

ADEWALE BRIGGS

***

*A*dewale Adegboyega Briggs is an Egba man from the East bank of the Ogun river, around a group of rocky outcroppings that rise above the surrounding wooded savanna, Abeokuta. To this day it is unclear who Adewale's biological Father is. His claim to Egba land is a consequence of his mother's lineage. Idowu Bolatito Briggs, the only daughter of her parents and the only sister to four boys was a wild child in her day. She got pregnant at twenty-two, had the baby, a boy and left for England shortly afterwards to study and start a new life. Her little boy was named Adewale Adegboyega by her parents. They raised him as theirs, as their last child and for the longest time, Adewale thought that Idowu was his elder sister who had always lived in the UK. He loved her dearly and often wished he had more sisters, even though they had the barest contact. Idowu seemed to be unavailable to not just Adewale but to her whole family. She hardly called and never came home to visit. It seemed like she had erased that part of her that read that she came from a family of seven turned eight. When she first left home, she would send things every month especially for Adewale. Toys, clothes, shoes, biscuits and chocolate. Adewale grew up fantasizing about one day meeting his dearly beloved elder sister who loved him so much; maybe even travelling with his mum to visit her. But none of that ever happened. Idowu never called nor came back. Her parents had thought initially that when she was done with school she would send for her son and make a life for both of them. Adewale always thought he had been told, or he had heard from some place, or he probably imagined it that he could start to visit his elder sister on his long holidays and eventually move to live with her. But Idowu had other plans. She had really bought into the idea that Adewale was her mother's last child and that all he needed from her were a few clothes, shoes, toys, biscuits and chocolate, once a month.

Adewale Adegboyega was an extremely intelligent child. He got his first pair of reading glasses at age five because like his mother said, he was born with bad eyes. The small circle-shaped glasses earned him the nickname "Awolowo" in school, plus he was always top of his class. He was also very different from the other Briggs kids. He was brown skinned. Nothing out of the ordinary or enough to get him noticed, but next to the Briggs, he seemed like what the Yorubas will call *dúdú*. The Briggs where known in their neighborhood as ìdílé aláwọ` funfun, the white-skinned family. Boluwatife Aremu Briggs, Adewale's grandfather, is an albino who married Ibidun, a light skinned woman. Rumor has it that Ibidun's fair skin is more enhanced than it's natural, still, all their five children are light skinned the color of egg yolk. All, except the sixth,

Adewale.

The Briggs kids were known around their neighborhood in Aguda, Surulere as very social and outgoing children. Maybe a little wild and troublesome. From the Ìbejì, to Idowu and to the last two boys, they never shied away from a fight and most often were known to start one. However, this last child Adewale, was the furthest prototype from the Briggs children. He was bookish, clumsy, handy around the house, wore glasses and was socially inept. He liked to stay indoors and close to his mother. He never played street football with the other kids after school but preferred to go to Aguda market and stay with his mum at her wrapper and lace shop until she closed. Ibidun Jaiyeola Briggs adored her grandson-turned-son. Her husband was very worried that she would emasculate the boy. Adewale was always by his mother's side when he wasn't in school. He always helped her cook and clean. They went to the market together and attended church prayer meetings together. There were hushed rumors around the neighborhood that Ibidun had an affair; probably with a dark-skinned man that produced this son that was so different from her children with her husband. One would say because Boluwatife was not Adewale's father, he was more comfortable with him clinging to his mother, but Ibidun loved every bit of attention she got from Adewale. Everybody called him *àpamọwọ́ ìyá,* which means mother's handbag.

The first time Ibidun Briggs noticed something was amiss was about six months after their daughter, Idowu, left for London. She had started complaining to her husband about how less frequently Idowu called home and how detached she seemed about her son,

Adewale. He had told her that the girl was young and had not come to an understanding of what being a mother was. She was studying and may need sometime. But when they could not reach her on the number she gave them and she had not called in months, it was becoming clear to them that either something was wrong, or she had decided to cut off. But why would their only daughter cut off from her family and abandon her own child? When Idowu told her parents to name the child, they did not think anything of it. After all, parents in these parts, name their grand-children even in situations when the daughter was properly married. Every now and then, they would receive gifts from Idowu via courier but they had no way of reaching her because her phone number was always switched off. Ibidun's cousin, Folake, whom Idowu stayed with when she first moved to London did not know her whereabouts either, as Idowu had long moved out and cut off communication.

When Adewale was in secondary school, he travelled with his mother to London. To "stock up her shop" was the reason she gave him, but Ibidun was tired of wondering and even felt afraid that something sinister may have happened to her only daughter. What if she had died alone in her room and nobody knew?! Or a bad boyfriend had done something to her? All kinds of morbid thoughts she consciously tried to put out raced through her mind about her daughter and she was sick of it. She needed to know. She had to go and find her. Adewale had never experienced such cold in his entire young life. It was late November when they visited London. The snow was heavy and his lungs almost gave way. His mother had to constantly rub his growing chest and feet with Aboniki balm, underneath all the warm clothing before they went out. They stayed at Folake's flat for two weeks before returning to Nigeria. It was an uphill task looking for Idowu in London. Folake had heard that she was back in school for a master's degree. Her mother went to the school, left messages at her department and with colleagues that knew her. It was worrisome and heart breaking to Ibidun that she had to trail her daughter like a spy. Luckily, a night before their departure, Idowu showed up at her aunt, Folake's house.

She had no reaction when she saw her mother and Adewale but seemed rather irritated that her mother was running amok her school, leaving messages for her as though she was a missing person. Adewale had excitedly given her a hug, thanking her for all the things she sent to him over the years but quickly realized his beloved sister's aloofness. Being the sensitive boy that he was, he withdrew immediately. That night, Idowu and her mum had a bad fight. She was fine and didn't need her mother or anybody checking up on her like a child. She did not want the child or anything to do with him. Why else did she let them name him? He was their child and not hers. Ibidun did not recognize this stranger before her spewing all the gibberish. Where was her daughter and what had this alien done with her? "Táni bàba Adewale?" She asked her daughter while shedding silent tears. "Why have you never told us who the boy's father is, Idowu?" Suddenly mindful of her grandson, she motioned to Folake to close the door "Bámit'ilẹkùnyẹn Folake. Omobìnrinyìíti pa mí.""Aunty mi, e take e easy." Said Folake, attempting to calm her older cousin down."I don't want Adewale to hear you two shouting."Folake went on, visibly worried that Adewale would hear this unwelcome conversation. "Folake, báwonimọs'elè mu nìírọ̀rùn?" Ibidun replied."How can I take it easy? Can't you hear what this girl is saying? Omobìnrinyìíti pa mí.".".She raged on, stomping her feet on the ground like both her legs had been seized by the resolute power of a bad Charlie horse and slapping her laps simultaneously in the same manner Ramota, Jegede's wife in the drama New Masquerade, used to do. "Mummy ,ejọọ́. Ẹmábèère bàbá Adewale lọwọ́mi, because I don't know!" Idowu retorted, backing her mother with an ugly frown on her face."I don't want the boy!""O parọ́ Idowu Bolatito Briggs. Àyàfitóbáj'émikónimobí ẹ. You lie!" Her mother fired back, jumped to her feet and started pacing around the room. Slapping her chest now like a charged-up gladiator, she shouted repeatedly, "Except I'm not the one who gave birth to you, Idowu Bolatito Briggs. Májẹkín bú."On and on they went, until Idowu left in an angry fit. Ibidun had told her daughter she never wanted to see her again.

They left for Nigeria the next day and Adewale was never the same. His skin stayed the same while the difference snuck in through a pore and attached itself to whatever brittle part formed his center. If only both women knew the weight words carry, they might have given more value to silence. But it was too late. He had heard everything Idowu, whom he thought was his sister all the while, said to his mother who was suddenly now his grandmother. Disillusioned, he became detached, distant and preferred to be by himself. He started finding excuses not to stay home and went more on holidays to his friend's houses claiming they had one major project after another. He never asked his mother or anybody about what he had heard.

When Ibidun Jaiyeola Briggs passed away, Adewale had just finished secondary school. I guess the writer knew a thing or two when he said 'An apple doesn't fall very far from the tree.'He attended his grandmother's burial and then disappeared permanently, as Ibidun Jaiyeola Briggs had just done from their lives. He never spoke to or about Idowu his biological mother. He left home for good and moved in with his best friend's family in Ikeja, where he crossed paths for the first time with a certain vivacious twin called Tai Ajayi.

Adewale Adegboyega Briggs had always had the odds in his favour. He was best graduating student in all of his set and gained an Oxford scholarship to study in the UK. A victim of abandonment, Adewale unconsciously, projected the sameon his daughter,Yemisi.

CHAPTER FIVE
THE PARADOX

***

There are people placed on this earth, whose sole purpose is to show us how to live life and live it to the fullest, unapologetically too. Toluwalase Ayinde Makinwa is one of such people.

Fully human, fully flawed, fully alive and fully trying to be better every time. Tolu is my ex, but an ex is only really an ex when you don't fancy them anymore. I will always fancy Tolu. I met him at the Bank when I first moved back to Nigeria. I went to open an account and I was given these endless forms to fill at the customer service desk. Neck deep in my forms, this random guy walks up to me asking to use my pen. It was Tolu. "Excuse me, can I use your pen for a second to fill out this slip?" he said. "Of all the people in this banking hall today, you choose me to ask for my pen?" I said, looking up at this dark, slender, handsome six-footer. He smiled "You looked the most approachable?" He said, with that disarming smile playing across his face. I was the least approachable in the bank that day actually, hunched over those forms, reading glasses on with furrows between my eyes. "I'll take just a second, I promise." he said. I needed to get these forms done and leave for Ozumba Mbadiwe, but I caught the sarcasm he was throwing at me and I liked it. Moreover, with a smile like that, I was taken. It was the most beautiful smile I had ever seen. He had these set of white spaced out teeth. Nothing fancy, almost childlike but it found such a perfect fit on his face and made him completely irresistible to me when he showed them off in a smile. I handed him my pen submissively. He smiled again as he took it and something told me in that moment that he knew the effect that smile had and he used it well. I knew I was in trouble. Again, It seemed to me like he took his time with my pen and eventually came back to my corner and handed it to me. "Thank you." he said, but he wasn't making eye contact. "Yemisi." he added. I realized he was looking at my forms and had seen my name. "That's fast!" I said looking shocked. "You could just ask, you know?" I said. "I know, but I was trying to impress you." He said with that smile again. "I could ask for your number Yemisi but I've seen it already." He added. "Ok peeping Einstein, I am not impressed. At all." I said and made to get back to my forms. He was so amused and laughed so hard he collapsed in the seat next to me. "You've got jokes, I see." He added in between gasps of laughter. "I like you." he said tapping my shoulder like we were the oldest buddies ever. I was shocked at the sheer audacity of whoever this human was. "Wait, who are you again?" I asked him. "Oh! My bad, I'm Tolu." His hand extended for a hand shake. "Tolu Makinwa." He added. I did a quick eye roll and took his hand. "I saw that, by the way, Yemisi." he said playfully. "I intended for you to see it Tolu Makinwa." I said. I liked him already. He felt like someone I had known forever. From then onwards we started talking and hanging out non-stop, this Tolu and I. I was new to Lagos and I had very few friends back then, so I hung on to this Tolu liaison almost desperately.

Tolu and I are age mates, but his persona is nothing short of a paradox. He is unattached yet permanent. He doesn't want a commitment but he is extremely territorial. He presents himself like a truant, you'd probably pick him out as the most unserious person in any crowd, but he is razor sharp intelligent, kind of like a magnet of knowledge. Tolu is an IT Engineer who was working at Google UK before moving back to Nigeria two years before I did. He now works at MTN. Deeply spiritual and unapologetically carnal, Tolu is the most selfless lover there is out there, fullstop. Sex with him was like a day out at the spa. Full blown pampering. He aimed only to please and also enjoyed himself while at it. I remember fondly how he'd take his time to kiss my fingertips one after the other and then my palms ever so gently while his eyes never let go of mine. I found it very weird at first, very uncomfortable and even a little exposed the way he would stare with an aim of getting a reaction from me. I tried to control my reaction to this sensual act I found extremely pleasing, but not for long. He would say things like, "Misi, do you realize that music is the only sensual pleasure without vice?" "It's a vice if the wordings are lewd and it causes me to have impure thoughts that may lead me to sin." I would reply, knowing that what would proceed would be an everlasting argument. Needless to say, the friend chemistry / lover chemistry with Tolu was unmatchable and I thought naturally, that we were an item. You know, a couple.

I was wrong.

One Friday night, I left work late, got takeout from a Chinese restaurant and headed to Tolu's place. I had talked to him earlier about his Friday night plans and he had said he was staying in that night to work on some project, so I thought it would be perfect to go spend my Friday there since I didn't want to go out as well. I got there after a not-so-short-or-long traffic, tired with take-out in hand, only to find Tolu cozied up on his living room couch with this girl! She was wearing his shirt! (Ladies and gentlemen, I am using these exclamation marks just so you can understand my shock not only at Tolu's actions but at his sheer guts to even act this way!)

There they were, watching something on his laptop! They looked too comfortable. They definitely had had sex. That girl almost looked rumpled in an-I-have-just-rolled-in-the-hay kind of way. I hated her instantaneously. "Oh hey, Misi." Tolu said, looking up and going back to what he was watching, like we were cordial housemates. I was used to being acknowledged, maybe even revered by my men, so please understand dear reader, that all this nonchalance was too much for me. "Tolu, can I see you? In private." I said, looking as stern and as severe as I had never looked before. He reluctantly excused himself and came with me to his room. I was the girl who would never, ever give away her emotions over a guy in front of another girl. I just couldn't give them that kind of power. "What is that?" I asked him once the door was closed. "What is what?" he asked. "What is that in your shirt you're sitting with? Is that the so-called project?" I insisted, arms folded defensively in front of me. "Misi, stop being a bitch, it's not a good look on you.

That's Linda. A friend. I could have just introduced you two if you wanted to know." He said. "Don't tell me what to be Tolu. What is this? A patronize me session? I thought you and I were good. So you're just gonna be random with these, these scamps in and out of this place?" I was getting upset now. I actually allowed myself to think that Tolu and I were exclusive. I mean, a guy is not that great with you in all spheres and not want to keep you to himself right? Yeah, but just don't expect to keep him all to yourself. "First of all, Misi, you and I are good. But we're not exclusive, so drop the first lady act. I mean we're great together, but I'm not looking to be tied down or else I'd be married, innit? Besides, if you told me you were coming, I'd have told you Linda was here just so we can avoid any drama." He said. "First lady? Seriously, Tolu! Piss off!" I turned to go and he grabbed my arm. "Hey Misi, I'm sorry ok? I don't mean it like that. Ok I'll send her away. Will that make you happy?" he asked. "That may be a start. Dunno if I'd be happy though, I'm hard to please like that." I replied looking away from him and rolling my eyes. He left the room and told the girl in the living room he was going out, so see her some other time. She promptly dressed up and left. I was un corporative that night. We made out but I refused to have sex with him. I didn't want to be one of the girls he picked up and tossed out like bad eggs. But somewhere at the back of my mind, I thought, weren't we all the same? Me and the girl that had just been sent away like Hagar. I may feel special now because some girl was sent away on my account, but I could be next on the send-away list when he thinks he's had enough of me. Besides, was anything really done on my account? A few minutes after I got to Tolu's place, I was going to walk out in anger. He could have decided to let me go, but he chose not to. No, nothing was done on my account. We live in a man's world no doubt but that world is incomplete without women. It's actually empty without women. Women, we have so much power, yet it always seems like nothing is done on our account. From then onwards I never assumed what was not expressly said to me in my relationships.

The paradox of modern love is that the forces that bind us together, like trust, mutuality and friendship are the very things that kill our sex lives stone dead. I realise that with Tolu, I'll never build those forces at the deepest level; maybe that's why the thrill remains with him. Erotic desire is often complex, messy and very often non-parental control, just like my relationship with Tolu. I officially assigned the title of friend-with-benefits to him in my head and I have struggled for him to be no more than that since then.

CHAPTER SIX
CAESAR IFECHUKWUADIGO ABEO BABATUNDE OKEKE

***

I've looked at these two sharp red lines in the window of this strip for the umpteenth time and it still doesn't make any sense to me. I cannot be pregnant. It's impossible. I have never missed a day on my oral contraceptives since I became sexually active. Oh my God! I'm even more mortified at the thought that it is Nomso's baby.

Chinomso William Okeke. We met at the Nigerian Bar Association (NBA) annual conference in Abuja some years ago. I could have cared less; he was a nice guy, simple and available. Absolutely not my type, but he made a great distraction. He was one of the lawyers at the legal department of First Bank Plc on Admiralty Way, Lekki phase 1 and was chosen to attend the conference holding at Abuja that year. He was cute and we flirted. He also insisted we keep in touch after we got back to Lagos. I obliged him sometimes when I was bored and feeling generous with my time, mostly because my life at that time consisted of three things, work, work and more work. Occasionally on some Saturdays, I'd spend time with Gogo and Trey, her son. Up until three months ago I was in a very complex relationship with 58-year old Ed. Full name: Edema Mark Agbeyegbe. Lagos socialite and top auditor at Deloitte. Ed is recently in couple's therapy with his wife because she woke up one day and was fed up with the lies and his philandering. She quietly packed up and left with their two children and the dog while he was at work. You know a woman means business when she acts with no notice, in pitch perfect silence. No clues or signs that she was angry or that something was wrong. Ed almost ran mad when he came back to a house devoid of his family and an address of their location. Awele Agbeyegbe had blocked his number and refused him any contact with her or the kids for two consecutive weeks. After this, she gave him her first condition; couple's counseling three days a week and until she saw significant change, she wasn't coming back. Ed was desperate to get his life back and to prove to his wife that he could change. Needless to say, he sent me the most bizarre breakup text which read "It was nice knowing you. Goodbye." The nerve of that guy! He would actually win if this was a six worded essay contest but it wasn't. It was my life, sordid as fuck, but I know I deserved more than this telling brusqueness. At first, I wasn't going to call him, because I didn't even believe he was serious about breaking up with me. Then a few days later the small voice of doubt began to creep in. Maybe it was my fault? Is he with someone else? Maybe I need to tell him how much I love/hate him? Is he even missing me? Maybe I should call him.

Soon enough, doubting Thomas turned into a huge green

glittering snake exhorting me to eat the apple. I called up all his phones frantically for uncountable times until he blocked my number and I haven't been able to get to him for weeks. No explanations, nothing. I didn't even know why he broke things off until Lola heard the full gist from her cousin Mimi, who happened to be close friends with Awele Agbeyegbe. Ed was the perfect guy for me though, older, complicated, unavailable, intelligent, and sharp witted. Our relationship was sensual, cerebral, sexual, intense, yet light. Most of all, it was a boomerang affair; you know, those fight-and-break-up-today-then-come-back-stronger-than-a-nineties-trend-tomorrow type of delirious affairs. I think I was a little in lust with the man but not to the point where I couldn't let him go though. You know, I'm removed that way and I was the mistress that respected the wife's squatter's rights. I wish he trusted me enough to tell me about what was going on with him cos' no matter how into him I was, I wasn't there to end his "I do", trust me. I liked our arrangement perfectly. Ed was an honorable man. No matter where the throes of adultery took him and for the kind of deep conversations him and I had, he never mentioned his wife or kids and I thought that made me like him more. I mean, he never denied being married when we first met; he didn't have to. I guess in the end I was only worth six scrawny words! Now I see clearly how Tolu Makinwa would have felt.

I rebounded badly after Ed's break up. I was at Nomso's every night like a vigilante at his post and whether he wanted it or not, we had sex every single time. He thought I was a nymphomaniac and I didn't care to refute it. I felt a little sorry for the guy because he obliged my delirium. It's like there was this formless void I was trying to fill up with all that sex and sweat but the more I got it, the more I wanted it and upon that, I felt absolutely nothing! It was pointless and I didn't even have Lola and Gogo to make it all better like before. Marriage had created some weird distance between Gogo and I and even when I saw her and Trey on some Saturdays, I didn't feel the need to talk to her about my affairs anymore because I noticed that suddenly, my issues were a tiny speck compared to the mountain of marital problems she was having with Molade, with him not letting her be her full self. Bitch, bye! I tried to tell you then you were fake around him but no! I was the bad guy. Lola on the other hand, is always super busy these days. It's hard to even get her to talk for five minutes uninterrupted on the phone. It's funny, because even though Gogo and I were closer, Lola was actually the one I could really talk to about the heavy stuff, you know, all the emotional-figuring-out. We had a very comfortable rhythm like that. We hung out last about two months ago when she told me all I needed to know about Mr. Six-worded-break-up-text. Even then, our outing was cut short; one of her clients needed an impromptu style consultation. She has attained a well-deserved rock-star status in her line of work and I am so proud of her. Still, it doesn't help me to be friendless at this corner I have turned in my life right now.

It's funny how in the movies, grown women always seem to have their friends, their careers and all that going for them. It's a whole different story in reality. In reality, you and your friends take different paths, and you all don't seem to find the balance like they do in the movies. When one friend marries, there seems to be a shift of focus and rightly so, but I'm amazed at how we women lose ourselves and identities completely to these liaisons, so much that we have no time to take care of ourselves. I suppose in trying to build a family and a home, the builder relegates self-care. But I think the reason why the movies always make their female characters have a close friend or two is because genuine friendship is part of how a woman takes care of herself. A woman needs her friend/s. I'm talking about the real friends, not the fly-by-night traitorous types. I also realize that often times, these friends change as we move through life. If we're lucky enough, we stay stuck with the old ones. I always thought Gogo and I would weather any storm. That we would stay friends no matter what. But I was beginning to see a different side to her now that she was married. She never ever visited me. I always had to make out time to go see her and Trey. Gogo didn't work anymore after she married Molade. She didn't have to actually. She owned a clothing and jewelry store that practically ran on its own, whether she was there or not. I worked a 9 to 5 job, five days a week and I still made out some Saturdays to visit her. We talked only about her. If it wasn't Molade did this, it was Molade didn't do that. Molade, Molade, Molade! She never asked how I was doing. At least not seriously. I realized that her level of selfish couldn't be helped. The worst part was when I stopped calling or visiting her. That was it! She never called to find out how I was or anything. So that was the end of Gogo and I. The friendship was dependent on me for sustainability and I had no energy left to keep it going. Whereas, Lola surprised me. She was busier than I was, but somehow, she always sent me little updates via texts like "Just landed NY, POK about to take over. Your girl made it! How are you?"And we would yay and shout at her successes, any chance we got. Sometimes, she would call me at 3am to cry about a job gone rogue and we would talk till I had to go to work.

I mean, we saw like once in a decade maybe, but there was a care and a shatter-proof bond that I recognized. That's what I hold on to.

Lola's phone has been switched off for days now. She's probably not even on this continent. I suppose it's Mummy Kay to the rescue then.

Well, I'm married now with an infant son, so you know by now that telling Mummy Kay about the pregnancy was a wrong move or right move, whichever way you want to look at this. She went into beast mode the minute I told her about it and my decision to terminate. She flew back to Lagos the following week and insisted on immediately meeting Nomso, who was as clueless of the news as a pirate wearing two eye patches. In her characteristic brisk style, Mummy Kay planned the traditional and registry weddings within two weeks. I told her I didn't love Nomso, that he and I only had a 'thing'. She told me it didn't matter and that women didn't always marry for love. She added that Dolly Parton once said if you want the rainbow you've got to put up with the rain. I wasn't sure what that meant and what the country star legend had to do with my ovaries but, well….

Of course, when Nomso knew about the pregnancy, he went into one of those I-know-we've-been-doing-it-alot-but-I'm-certainly-not-the-only-man-you-are-sleeping-with mode. Fair enough, but then I told him I was three months in and the only other man I was seeing had called things off about five months back. I went on to say that I shouldn't even be pregnant since I was on an iron clad contraceptive. Moreover, I intended to terminate the pregnancy because I loved my free time. But my Mummy Kay wouldn't hear of it; she was on a the-baby's-life-must-be-saved-at-all-cost mission. After this revelation, Nomso activated his nothing-must-happen-to-my-baby mode. He went from threatening to sue me if I terminated the baby to proposing marriage and a lifetime of love and happiness, all in one sitting. I must confess, his attempt to save the baby's life was very cute, but I didn't need it or any other person's attempt for that matter, because Caesar Ifechukwuadigo Abeo Babatunde Okeke is my world and I can't believe that the possibility of not having him in my life ever crossed my mind. His paternal grandma named him Ifechukwuadigo, which means "God's light has come" in Igbo. Mummy Kay called him Baba Agba's middle name, Abeo and of course Babatunde, because she strongly believes that Baba Agba is reincarnated. I loved my grandfather dearly, but I don't want Caesar to be anybody else but himself. I want him to have his own strengths and his own flaws and his own life, devoid of us connecting his every move to someone else's, even if that person was my beloved Baba Agba.

It wasn't love at first sight for us, that's for sure. No sudden burst of love or anything like they portray in the movies or books. I felt like somebody had left their baby with me and I wasn't sure of my next move. I was very curious about him and a little afraid while he just stared at me with eyes wide open, cried when he needed to and slept. He was very light skinned like Nomso's dad. I definitely wasn't ready for the worry armor that indelibly strapped itself around me like the skin I couldn't get rid of. I had read stories about babies choking in their cradles, rolling over and suffocating and that shit kept me up at night, watching this little creature like a hawk, I swear. These days I can't even cuss without feeling like I am corrupting his pure little ears! Have I told you how terrified I felt being left alone with him? It was real life fear, no joke! I wasn't always sure I was doing the right thing. We basically always had a stare down, he and I, which he always broke with a smile, followed by a chuckle and then he would roll over casually. He made me fall in love with him, with his calm non-verbal gestures. He was a very tranquil baby with an aura of maturity about him. He cried only when he was hungry or uncomfortable and never wildly. He was nothing like me and I almost felt sometimes like I was the child and he the adult. He gave a good stare though, almost like he was studying his subjects from his onesie-clad little throne. I had never ever experienced anyone or thing like this.

I moved back to London when I was seven months in and that raised hell at work. The firm manager expected me to keep working till the last day of the eighth month, then go have the baby and be back after three months, which meant that I legit had only two months' maternity leave. Talk about the bitch called the private sector. You remember the smallest man alive, Oris Kingsley Ejidawe aka Oke? Yeah, he's the firm manager now, so imagine all the petty hoops I'd have to jump. I wasn't having any of that. I went to HR with my application for a six-month leave outside of my maternity leave without pay, as long as my job was waiting for me on my return. I can't come and kill myself.

Mummy Kay made sure Caesar and I had the best care in the world. Over the years after the Timothée situation, Mummy Kay never played house with anybody again. As a matter of fact, I hardly met any of her dates again as I was conveniently off to boarding school, university and eventually Nigeria. Mummy Kay went back to school and eventually became a Certified Registered Nurse Anaesthetist (CNRA). I kid you not, that's boss lady status right there. She now worked at St. Thomas' Hospital on Westminster Bridge Road, where I delivered Caesar with the best care ever. She had also moved into this beautiful, all white walls, two-bedroom condo, in a nice quiet neighborhood. Mummy Kay was ecstatic at Caesar's birth. She kept reciting "Bàbá káàbọ̀" (welcome father) and dancing round with the baby. Then she was suddenly crying, wishing that Baba Agba and Taiwo Ajayi Briggs were alive to see this day. I did wish my grandfather was alive to meet Caesar though. He would have been so proud, he would have bought the whole world for the baby. Baba Agba had suffered a series of health issues in the last days of his life and it was almost a relief for me when he passed on. I hated seeing him suffer so much. Caesar and I stayed with Mummy Kay for over six months and now I know old man Dickens knew a thing or two when he said 'it was the best of times, it was the worst of times.' The best because Mummy Kay and the full squad of nurses and midwives made having a baby less scary, the worst of times because for the first three months of his life, Caesar was an insomniac at night and slept like a log through the day. Thoughts of finding a suffocated baby lying on his nose in the morning kept me on vigilante mode at night and utterly useless during the day. Mummy Kay worked only on night shifts for all the time we were in London. During the day, Caesar and I slept mostly from our night vigils, but Mummy Kay would wake him in between naps to feed, cuddle, and sing to him until he fell asleep again. By the time he and I got back to Nigeria, I had learnt everything I needed to know about caring for him. I wasn't afraid anymore to be alone with him because I was now more confident about what I was doing and I felt ready, armed with the fierce indisputable love torch I now carried for my little man and with everything Mummy Kay, the midwife and the neonatal nurses had taught me about baby care and self-care.

What I however wasn't ready for was the cureless Lagos traffic. The ride from the airport to the house took almost more than half the day. The fact that Nomso and I hadn't really lived together before made everything so new and surreal. I was so used to focusing only on Caesar, but suddenly, I had to add a grown man to my worry list. I wasn't prepared for Nomso's expectations of me as a wife and worst of all, I hated the servitude our marriage placed on me. Nomso had expressly told me he could neither cook nor clean when I first met him. When I would stay over at his house then, we would order take outs and his kitchen was always spotless, save for when we would warm up the food or soup he ordered regularly from a caterer. He would joke then that his wife had to really love cooking because he couldn't do it even to save his life. At Mummy Kay's house when Timothée lived with us, he did all of the cooking simply because he loved to cook. Mummy Kay or I would do the dishes afterwards, depending on who was free. But sometimes, Timothée did the dishes even after he cooked. He was a hands-on guy around the house and about everything. Mummy Kay didn't have to ask for help to get it. It was an unspoken rule that Timothée did the work around the house along with Mummy Kay. The reverse was the case in my marriage. I cooked, cleaned up, did the laundry and tended to all of Caesar's needs with barely any help from Nomso. It's either I didn't know how to ask for help or my pride wouldn't let me, so I carried on doing everything like a super woman that I am not. Even when I gathered up the courage to ask for his help, he always hid behind his bank job, quoting his endless working hours and claiming he was too tired to help. We had the most ferocious arguments. I just couldn't understand this whole African-man-on-his-ego-throne-act Nomso was exhibiting. I never thought he would be the kind of man that would refuse to be hands-on or even learn to become one. I wasn't ready for this life. I had a job, a baby, my newly found asexuality and an impossible marital *situationship*. I think it would have been a lot easier if I was in love with Nomso. I wasn't and it was even more magnified, now that we were married. The mythical scene which often goes something like this – I'm trudging along in life, lonely but coping, some enchanted evening in a crowded room, I meet the perfect stranger aka Nomso (as opposed to a total stranger), fade in music, fade out loneliness, I'm lifted to this pinnacle of bliss, where me and Prince Nomso Charming live happily ever after – was not to be our story (if it's even anybody's story!). I married Nomso because I was pregnant by him. My life was empty; there was no Gogo or Lola to fall back on and my older men liaisons were getting fickle by the count. Nomso and I didn't date or court before this commitment and I can't say I knew enough about him to become his wife, neither did he know enough about me to propose. What we had was a *sexationship,* aka we have sex, no feelings involved and we go our separate ways. But I think that people fall for you when you are being absolutely mindless and that's how Nomso fell for the wrong girl, me. I had no business accepting his marriage proposal; he is absolutely not my type, but I let Mummy Kay convince me to marry him because somewhere at the back of my head, my first act of selflessness was to make Caesar's father and us a family. This decision has been the toughest bone I've had to chew. For starters, motherhood has lent me a certain gravitas that is a surprise even to me. Unlike my dear husband, I have zero interest in clubbing/partying and unnecessary social outings now. Even worse, I have no interest in fleshly things. I think motherhood has turned me asexual. My skin crawls at Nomso's touch and I told him I needed time. Poor thing! I think he thought it was the same nymphomaniac Misi, pre-Caesar. It isn't. Much to my surprise, I have changed 180 degrees since Caesar's arrival and it would take a deeper connection to get me excited in any way now. I just want to work, earn and take care of my baby and it just feels like Nomso is in the way of that. It feels like he is in the way of everything, phew!

We fight about everything. He thought I should exclusively breastfeed Caesar for a year. I alternated breast milk with baby formula because at the time of Caesar's birth, my breast milk production was too low for the wolf-like appetite Caesar had. Nomso wanted us to resume sex immediately I got back and when I turned down his advances three times in a row, he called Mummy Kay who in turn called me for an hour's lecture on how to "keep my man happy". Nomso refused to use a condom when sex nights fell on my ovulating days. He asserted that I should go and get on one of the family planning *thingys* or better still, that he would "pull out" on time before he spilled. Seriously? Like what are we? Teens?

This is going to be harder than I actually envisaged.

I lost my job at Akin Thomas, Hollaway and Gibson LLP by the way. When Oke found out in my absence that I had overridden his authority and gone to HR with my six-month leave without pay application, he went straight to the partners with an we-need-to-hire-active-hands-and-fire-redundant-ones-memo, stating that the company could not afford the duration of "leave-takers" even if it was without financial remuneration. He cited the premise that it was post-election period in Nigeria at the time and the firm was swamped with election petitions. He made a pretty strong case if I may say so myself, and that was it! On my first day of resumption, I was given a letter that read in part"........due to the back log of cases the firm is presently dealing with, it became paramount in your absence to grant employment on a temporary basis, pending the probationary duration, to three lawyers in the capacity of Junior Associates. Consequent upon this development, the firm no longer requires your services as Senior Associate, effective immediately. The firm however, based on the long standing relationship it has established with you, would like to offer you a retainership position only at your inst....."

'Bastards!' I didn't have to read the whole garbage. After over 10 years of hard work and sweat and putting up with God-knows-what, this is what I get? A bloody retainership for I'm sure, a quarter of my monthly pay. I yelled at the glass that walled my office. That explains the weirdness about everybody at the office when I got in this morning and how they all seemed to avoid eye contact with me. They must all have had prior knowledge of this grand sack slash retainership bullshit, as I was also very certain they were all watching me while I read my letter and rail through their glass walls. "Gossips, the whole bunch of them!" I thought to myself. Akin Thomas, Hollaway and Gibson was a whole building of glass, little wonder it was bereft of any secrets. And for lawyers who should be about the law, we sure had time on our hands to be about everybody else's business. God knows I didn't need that any more.

Life as Misi Okeke is no less complex and it's dawning on me that I didn't have to marry Nomso. Having a baby with someone does not equals marrying them. Gosh! why did I let Mummy Kay talk me into marriage. All her the-baby-deserves-to-have-both-mother-and-father-around-in-one-house talk seems less convincing now that I am living in a marriage devoid of a job and passion. I mean, Nomso is a good guy don't get me wrong, but there is something to be said about when a guy just doesn't light your fire. This script I am playing with him is boring the wind out of me. But I am trying. For Caesar's sake I am. To make our lives work, Nomso and I now have sex at least once a week usually on the weekend but only on my non-ovulation days because he is adamant on his non-use of condoms. Moreover, given these cancer times we live in, I have refused to put any foreign objects or ingest any hormonal medication on account of family planning. I mostly lie on my back and make all the appropriate faces and noises until he is done. When I am really in the mood however, I make out time to be alone at the house and have a good ol' session with my vibrator. I hired a maid to clean, cook and do all the servitude that Nomso requires. I put Caesar in a crèche so I can have some me-time during the day and also job hunt.

Things are looking up again. My application for a job at a very small law firm, Rhodes Legal, is gaining traction. A commercial law firm on Awolowo Road, Ikoyi. I have been called for a second interview for the position of Junior Associate. It will pay me a little over half of my salary at Akin Thomas and Co., but half bread they say is better than none. The firm is close to my house and Caesar's crèche, I will be gainfully employed and earning, unlike somebody I know! What's not to like? My plan is to start at Rhodes Legal, when I get hired and search for greener, better pastures. Fingers crossed.

CHAPTER SEVEN
THE IN-LAWS

***

*C*hinomso William Okeke is the older of the two children of his parents, Dr. Albert Ikenna Okeke and Adaobi Augusta Okeke. His younger sister, Chizaram, famously called Zara, married a very wealthy politician and has never approved of her brother's association with me. I've always wondered if this enormous vitriol of hers doesn't stem more from jealousy than good reasoning.

You see, Zara and her husband of many years have been trying to have children to no avail, while I waltzed my way into the Okeke family with a baby in tow. She and Nomso share a very close and secure bond and she can easily influence him. So can Mrs Okeke their mother. Zara always said Nomso was made for more and could do better than marrying "ofemmanu", a derogatory term used by the Igbo's in reference to the Yoruba's, that literally means "oil soup". Needless to say, Zara is not my greatest fan. I personally think it's understandable that she would feel jealous that some other woman would hold her brother's full attention so well - something she is clearly incapable of doing not just with her brother but with any man. Quite frankly, I never lose sleep over anything Zara. I have too much on my plate to take a spoilt tribalistic brat's tantrums to heart.

Mrs. Okeke, on the other hand, is a more irenic, quiet and thoughtful lady. A Professor of English at the University of Nigeria Nsukka, Prof. A.A Okeke, as she is fondly called around the university community, is an Oxford trained Professor and I suspect she was and still is a great catch to the men of her generation. Slender and tall with a very delicate frame, she speaks English with a proper British diction just as well as she speaks her Igbo with the proper Igbo intonation. Prof A.A Okeke and her family, except for Zara of course, come across as very detribalized decent people. She is a little unconventional in her ways, which to me is refreshingly surprising.

When Nomso and I agreed to get married, we travelled to Nsukka to meet his parents. I'd never forget what Mrs. Okeke said to me then and I wish I had given it more attention. She looked at me for what seemed like the longest time and then said, "Yemisi, only choose in marriage a man whom you would choose as a friend if he were a woman. I hope my son is that man." I never forgot those words and at the time, I didn't even know Nomso well enough to know if I'd choose his feminine reverse. All I knew was that I was pregnant, tired and I wanted my baby to be born in a proper setting, with a father who was present, alive and willing to be a father. I wanted my baby to have better than I did. When I decided to keep the baby, that was the only reason I had in choosing to marry

Chinomso William Okeke.

Mrs. Okeke's version of the famous "omugwo" (the Igbo name for a customary practice in Nigeria where the grandmothers of a new born baby visit the family in turns to help with the baby for at least three months) was arriving Lagos with a hired nurse all the way from Nsukka. Nurse Ugonna was one of the best nurses in Nsukka and a long-term friend of the Okeke's. Nomso's mum openly admits with a laugh that she can't remember a thing about baby care. She had told Nomso prior their arrival to make reservations for two at the guesthouse a few blocks away from our house, claiming that new parents needed their space. They spent the whole day at our house however. Ifeadigo (her favourite name for Caesar) stayed home from his crèche for the duration of his grandmother's stay with us. When she first met Caesar on her arrival, she carried him, looking lovingly at his face as though she was searching for treasure and announced to Nomso, the nurse and I rather theatrically, "He is Ifechukwuadigo, God's light which has come to us and he will call me his Bebe. He will usher in all my grandchildren.""Amen!" Nurse Ugonna yelled so loudly that Caesar began to cry. From then on, we called Nomso's mum Bebe. Caesar being her first grandchild, she doted over him and practically bought the whole world for him. Toys he couldn't even play with at the time, a whole suitcase of baby clothing of varying sizes, a bag full of pull up diapers of varying sizes, a carton of Aptimil baby milk, a carton of baby wipes, everything. She cooked all our meals for the one week she was in Lagos, while nurse Ugonna cleaned, bathed Caesar and did his laundry. Nomso absolutely loved it when his mum visited us, but I think I enjoyed her visits a little more than him. You can tell he has been spoilt in the you-are-the-man-of-the-house type of way. That all too familiar and unfortunate throne where Nigerian parents carefully place their boy children, treating them like they were the holiest of holies, like if they were treated any less, they would decide to vanish from the earth and maybe appear in a more favorable home, tending to their every whim. The attitude consequently deprives them of that marrow that makes a man a hunter, a go-getter. They grow up thinking the world owes them, they are unchallenged, unable to stand on their own two feet. I don't think that Bebe set out to spoil their heir apparent, however, she understands tradition and culture and dare I say, a man's place in the Igbo culture. In trying to build a confident, well rounded Nomso and being the loving mother that she is, she probably over did it.

There are people who come into your life unexpectedly, when you're not looking and all they do is bless you. I think Bebe is one of such people. The thought of having a mother-in-law never crossed my mind because I never really thought that marriage was for me in the first place. When marriage eventually counted me in, I was utterly terrified at the idea of having a mother-in-law. Gogo had told me how scary Molade's mum was. The subtle cruelties, the catty remarks that shrouded feigned smiles and exaggerated laughter, all adding to her woes. My inability to connect with women, mostly older women, was my darkest dread about having a mother-in-law. When I first met Bebe, our connection was the most natural thing, much to my surprise. She just has a calm vibe about her. When she visited us after Caesar was born, she encouraged me to stay at work later if I had to and get back on my exercise routine at least for the time she was around. She would often say, "Having a baby isn't a death sentence Misi, it's supposed to make your life a little richer and fuller." Her conversations were very light, yet very cerebral and I suspect that she got to know a little more about you after those her casual converse. Adaobi Okeke is as sophisticated and as organic as they come, dignified and proper like a strand of pearls and the best thing that happened to me since I met my husband.

CHAPTER EIGHT
GROUND ZERO

***

*R*hodes Legal, the small corporate firm I mentioned earlier hired me, despite my criminal law specialty. Unbeknownst to the general public that a general law firm and a corporate law firm differed, people walked in everyday with criminal cases or civil cases to prosecute. Situated in a cardinal part of Ikoyi, the firm started thinking quickly about expansion and morphing from 100% corporate duties to omnibus. The Hiring Partner said casually at my second interview that based on my work experience and reference from A.T Holloway and Gibson, I was most likely the one to head the proposed litigation department at Rhodes. This however would not be automatic; it will depend on how well my cases went. John Adelomo Esq. was hired shortly after to oversee the civil cases. Ultimately, no wins, no litigation department. John and I had to bring our A-game; we had to make a certain percentage of wins within a certain duration of time to get the department started and things had kicked off pretty smoothly.

While I thrived at work, my relationship with Nomso deteriorated. More so, he had recently lost his job when his bank merged with two others. After the first few months of staying at home, Nomso became gravely distant and irritable. A couch potato to say the least, he ate all his meals in front of the TV, wouldn't take a bath, wouldn't shave, wouldn't go out to look for another job and wouldn't clean up. He soon stopped giving me money for our upkeep, claiming that he didn't have any to give. I was getting very impatient and very upset, so I called Bebe and told her what was going on. She invited her son to Nsukka for a week. When he got back from that visit he seemed more spirited and rested. More importantly, he started going out job-hunting and even socially with his friends. Bebe has a knack for getting the best out of anybody.

Zara's husband asked Nomso to move to Abuja and become his Personal Assistant for the time being, while he scouted around to find him a suitable job, but Nomso turned down the offer. I was livid. His reasons for turning it down will make even you upset. From, wait for it,...... "I am not keen on the PA thing and catering to every whim of a grown man doesn't appeal to me.", to "I am not ready to live away from my family or leave Lagos." It was impossible to convince Nomso to take the PA job. We had long angry arguments about his refusal to take the job. During one of such arguments he blurted, "You know Misi, this is all so convenient for you isn't it?" "What do you mean by that?" I asked rather irritably. "It all makes sense now. You wanting me out of Lagos so badly so you can go back to those cat daddies of yours". He was waving a finger in my face and slitting his eyes at me like Cinderella's evil step mum. He wasn't done. "After all, when I met you, you were all over Lagos with all kinds of old married farts. Who is to say you have stopped anyway?"That earned him an open palm slap across the face followed by a cold hard silence for the rest of the month, even after he had apologized. The cheek of him! Here I was, spending my salary and my savings every month, trying to keep us afloat while this bastard sits on the couch assessing my life with the concept of adultery. What he said hurt me deeply; that he would think I was still about the cat daddy life didn't hurt me as nearly as the thought that I was dating them for their money. Now there was the insult. Don't get me wrong, I'm not out here judging anybody, man or woman, that dates another for money. Your life, your rules! But I've always been the girl with her own money. I'd never wanted anybody to own me like that. Most of my "cat daddies" according to Nomso were generous and spoilt me with gifts, trips and money, but I also dated a lot of them that were not so generous and their stinginess was never the reason for our break-up. As a younger girl, Baba Agba and Mummy Kay made sure I always had money. Even now, she had started sending me money every other month since I had told her how hard things had become for us financially. She often said it was upkeep money for her grandson Babatunde, but I knew that was her way of helping me out. I had dated all those people in the past in search for something that was always changing, something I didn't even know. Sometimes I think I was looking for company, then I'd soon be searching for wit. Other times I thought I was looking for acceptance, then my search will change again to fun. Most times however, it just came down to good ol' sex. My shrink back in the UK, Prof. Luke Allen, explained it to me that I dated older men who were unavailable, especially emotionally and physically. These men he said, mirrored my father and I would seek them out, most often unconsciously, because that was what I was comfortable with. I was seeking for my unavailable dad, his love and his approval. I remember Prof. Allen saying that I was somewhat the poster-child of daddy-issues and I also remember not liking that title.

Bebe had recently sent money to Caesar's crèche for his two month's tuition and had also given Nomso money for our rent before it expired. But for how long were we going to depend on Caesars grand mums? I needed Nomso to get into his big boy pants sooner. I wasn't going to uproot my son and I from Lagos to go sit at home in Abuja with an unwilling PA, but I needed him to show some commitment. Being around Zara's husband would not only have him earning a monthly salary to send home, it would actually show the politician how committed and serious he is about getting his dream job. Who knows, he may start the PA job and actually enjoy it and maybe even make a career of it. The possibilities were endless. But no, Nomso preferred to stay home and let our mothers pay for his life while I slave away to pay for the rest.

We lived like two jealous co-wives in one house. Each avoiding carefully the other, while carrying on with our daily activities in silence.

One day, I was feeling saturated about my marriage, so I called Mummy Kay to pick her brain on what to do. While I was telling her of my frustrations with Nomso she cut in, "Dúpẹ́ fúnohuntí o ní Yemisi, kí odẹ́kunkíkùn. We need to focus on the good in our lives and be more appreciative omo mi." "It's hard to be appreciative in pain, mummy." I said. "Being a woman is hard Yemisi my daughter." She said quietly. "It's harder than life itself. You just have to find a way to make it bearable."

I think there is a pressure on people to always turn every negative into a positive; the pressure that doesn't allow you feel your negative feelings or talk about them. I wanted to be allowed to say I was going through something strange and it was altering me, or better still, I wanted my Mummy Kay to just listen to me rant, even if she didn't have any solutions for me. I now lived an unrelenting groundhog day of laundry, shopping, work and rearing Caesar. Twenty-four hours a day was no longer enough for me.

One day while I was at work, this pretty dark model-like girl walked in and said she wanted to sue somebody for sexual harassment at her work. She was an administrative staff in the Director's office at one of Lagos State's ministries at Alausa and the new person appointed as her Director wanted a piece of anything female in the building. Abeni Coker would stand out of any crowd, especially a civil service crowd. She was six feet tall, slender with a very polished dark skin - the color of midnight skies - pretty face, with lean features. And she dressed very well too! Nothing like what you find in the government ministries. She had worked as a runway model for some years until she got pregnant by a boyfriend who didn't like her decision to keep it. Needless to say, she couldn't get back on the runway soon enough and things became very tough. Her uncle got her the job at the ministry with the hope that she would find a 'decent' man and settle down. "No man wants to marry a naked woman, Abeni.", he would say about her modeling. She was commonly called Agbani everywhere. She was very witty and almost playful, but tempered, like somebody who was formally trained in the art of making friends. I hadn't met anybody like her since Gogo and Lola. I could tell we would be instant friends, but right now, I needed to be her lawyer. During her briefing, she told me that her Director was blatant with his harassment, despite the fact that she had turned down his advances severally. He would grab her buttocks in his office, address her by very lewd names and brush up against her. She had stopped going into his office and would ask her male colleagues to take and receive files from the Director's office on her behalf. When he noticed this, he specifically assigned the task of taking and receiving files to and from his office to Abeni. He would literally chase her around his desk in an effort to kiss her and it seemed like he was enjoying it. She had told him severally that she was not interested in having an affair with him to no avail. Rather, he said he loved a hard-to-get game because he always won in the end. He addressed her as Margaret Thatcher before her colleagues and threatened to sack her more than a few times. Abeni had put in her resignation at the ministry barely two weeks before she walked into my office that day.

I was building Abeni's case around the provisions of Chapter 4 section 34 of the Nigerian Constitution that guarantees the right to dignity of the human person and the criminal law of Lagos State 2011, which criminalizes sexual harassment with an imprisonment term of three (3) years. I was going to eat that Director alive in court with this and I was elated, but first, I needed Abeni to go back and start a documentation of this harassment. To my surprise and delight, she had audio recordings of her former boss talking dirty to her on her phone. She also had explicit text messages from him even after she had resigned. In addition, one of her former colleagues was willing to testify as a witness for her. It was going to be a walk in the park. When I was done with him in the criminal court, Adelomo was going to file a civil suit against him at the National Industrial Court at Ikoyi. All of this litigation was going to cost her a lot of money and I was a little worried that she could not afford that on a now-resigned bank account, so I suggested that we give the Director, whom I was certain would want to protect his reputation and name at all cost, the option of settling out of court. That way, we could take a percentage of the settlement fee as our remuneration while she got something for herself as well. But Abeni didn't want to settle out of court. According to her, any man with money could do his worst to any girl and then run under the cover of his money to settle out of court easily. She recounted how fearful she would feel every time and everyday she had to go to work or go into the Director's office. She had resigned because she knew the cruelty she would face from the Director and his sycophants, if he were suddenly served with court summons with her as the complainant. She wouldn't be able to withstand the hate. "No, he has to face the consequences of his actions so that no one else would ever experience this fear that became part of my life." she said with a defiant distant look on her face. I was so proud in that moment to be her lawyer and her friend. Abeni wanted the full wrath of the law on her former boss and that was what we were going to bring down on him. I wondered though, how this now resigned civil servant would afford such heavy litigation fees by herself. That was when she told me she had another job she did at night. One that paid her five times more than what she made at the ministry. Wow! I was curious and instantaneously very cautious. A night job that paid that good certainly had dodgy written all over it. Maybe she was the secret service police or a high-end courtesan. Lord knows I couldn't add hoe drama to my already turbulent life right now. "No, don't be silly Misi." she giggled playfully. "I'm not a prostitute. I'm a dancer. I entertain and create the wildest fantasies for men, that's all." "Ok." I said slowly, summing her up as if I could get the truth if I looked hard enough. She told me that she danced at a place called Ground Zero every night and as far as the ordinary Lagosian is concerned, this place does not exist. There are exclusive spots in Lagos State, Ground Zero is the exclusive of those exclusive spots. Owned by an unnamed top power player in Nigeria, this world-class gentlemen's den is built one storey into the earth and entertains the elite and most powerful men in and outside the country. Ground Zero initially admitted members-only, but lately, it has opened its doors, but I still won't say to the general public, because not anybody even with a truck load of money could get into this place. Access was mostly based on referrals or public recognition, but of course, one had to be recognized publicly for the right reasons to be admitted into Ground Zero. Ground Zero was to lounges what a three-star Michelin restaurant was to restaurants. "So you dance? For that much? What kind of dance is that Abeni?" I had so many questions. She leaned in a little with one open palm over her mouth like she was about to reveal the Davinci code. "Haha, sensual and sexual dance you know, that make guys hot." she whispered with a hearty giggle and a wink. I was assessing her while we talked and she seemed to me like someone who always aimed to shock her audience with the things she said. I looked confused and then she said with a faked exhausted look on her face "Ok Misi, have you watched Hustlers?" she asked and then winked at me playfully. "YOU MEAN STRIPPER DANCE?!" I yelled with my eyes bulging wide. "Shuuuuu." Abeni stretched her endless arms from her side of the table and covered my mouth with her hand. "You're shouting, Misi. We cannot talk about my work here. It's exclusive you know?"She said, looking around like we were in a room full of people. "Your work? You're a stripper?" I asked gazing at her, full-eyeball-size. "Yes, I am. And you say that like I'm the devil's assistant." "I'm sorry Abeni, if my reaction comes across as *judgy*. That is not my intent. But how are you ok with all those creepy old men touching you?" I said, trying hard to hide my shock. "Touching who? Wọn ò tóbẹ̀."She went on, "Misi, nobody touches me or any of the girls for that matter while we dance. Even the men that pay for private dances have a limit to what they can do on the lounge premises. Wait, you've never been to a proper gentlemen's lounge, right? Not all these nonsense ashewo clubs oh! I mean a proper den with professional dancers?" "No, I have never been." I said while shaking my head almost regrettably. I noticed that she never called it a strip club and she never referred to herself as a stripper. "Let's talk over lunch sometime Misi, I've got to run. Love to the little king." She stood up, all 6ft long and kissed the airs around my ears like the French do. She referred to Caesar as the little king. She hadn't met him physically but had fallen in love with him through the stories I told her of him and through his pictures on my phone and on my desk. How was this girl a stripper? This classy, soft-spoken, well-educated ex-model. She was a graduate of Political Science from the University of Ibadan and had the grace of a gazelle.

In the months that followed, Abeni became a regular guest at my office, not just for her case but we became fast friends just like I had suspected. She, single and ready to mingle and I, searching for a distraction from my groundhog-day life, sought out exciting new spots in Lagos on Saturdays. That was Abeni's day off as a "dancer" and weekends were my days off from lawyering. She told me she was known as Ben in ground zero and that the only person or thing that knew her real name in that world was her employment contract. All the dancers used aliases and most of the girls, she suspected, had every day jobs and were everyday people. "Aren't you afraid of being recognized outside the club by those men?" I asked her "And by the way, I'm calling you Ben from here on." I added. "Call me whatever you like babes. This one you are asking me all these questions *sef*, are you thinking of joining us?" Ben answered with her usual chuckle. "I am just curious actually." I said, reflecting. "But would it be so bad if I joined? I mean the pay will be everything I need right now, plus I've always wanted to dance." I added after a while, surprising Ben and even myself. "Ah! And what are you going to tell Nomso you are doing on nights when you dance? Ah! Misi ,fi mí sílẹ̀ o, mi ò fẹ́ wàhálà."She added, suddenly looking worried. "Let me worry about my husband Ben. Besides, maybe if he was working I wouldn't have to do a night shift to support us!" I said in phony anger. "That's it! A night shift job." I said with my eyes lighting up. "Hold up! Madam night shift! " Ben said with both hands up in the air, mimicking surrender. "You know I have to convince my manager on why he has to hire you right? This place is not a walk in the park Misi. You've got to earn your slot there and be on your A-game, no joke." "Ah ah! Abeni, I mean Ben. Why are you talking like you don't know your girl now? But come oh! What if somebody I know recognizes me?" I asked suddenly worried. "Babes, nobody can recognize you in those costumes we have on, with masks, frails, tails and the whole bit. Don't worry about that." Ben said. "What you should worry about is what your husband will do when he finds out what exactly this "night shift" is all about.",she added, making inverted commas in the air with both hands."He can only find out if somebody tells him. That somebody will have to be either me or you and I know I'm not telling. Are you?" I asked.

CHAPTER NINE

DOWN THE RABBIT HOLE

***

*N*othing Ben said could have prepared me for Ground Zero. Nothing I say to you now can fully describe what this place is. It's one of those places you need to experience for yourself. Ben had told the Lounge Manager, who was called Uncle, about me and he asked to see me. I was to come with my CV and two passports, which would be used for my documentation, if I passed the interview. Ground Zero girls aren't just any girls. They are all well-schooled with BScs and BAs. They are trained on Ground Zero grounds in dance, finesse, likeability and general etiquette. These girls are make-you-feel-good professionals. Now I understand why I liked Ben instantaneously when we met. They are trained to make you like them.

Ben and I met up with Uncle at Ground Zero on a Saturday morning when the lounge was empty and quiet, so I really took in the sights of it. I'm not sure what I expected this "Uncle" character to look like, but I remember feeling so nervous and excited at the same

time that the whole visit became an out-of-body experience. Uncle
turned out to be Notorious B.I.G's doppelgänger, complete with
the humongous framed glasses. But his glasses were clear and not
shades like the dearly departed. He was surprisingly soft spoken,
but there was an up-tightness behind his persona that inspired a
brand of respect. With a size and look like his, I doubt that any
human or animal for that matter would want to get on his wrong
side. There was a veneer of hardcore toughness buried just-below-
the-surface, underneath all that chubby mass and he looked you
straight into the eyes even after you had answered his question as if
he was waiting for you to come up with the actual answer, or as if he
was deciding whether you were lying or telling the truth. If you
have watched the Fantastic-Four movie, then you must have seen
"The Thing" (Ben Grimm). There were two The-Thing-like men
planted at the entrance and exit of this lounge. If you haven't
watched the Fantastic-Four movie, then the only way I can describe
these men are a swollen mass of muscles, like extreme weight lifters
on steroids dressed military-style in black khaki's and grey t-shirts.
Their necks, arms and limbs seemed thicker than Iroko tree trunks.
Their combat khaki pants were tucked in at the ankle into their
black timberlands boots and they had on black wholly gloves and
wireless head microphones. They had LED search sticks attached to
their khaki pants like bag charms and Ben said they even carry stun
guns in their pockets, in case anybody got out of order. They didn't
move or speak to us when we arrived because my guess is, Uncle
had informed them to let Ben and her guest, aka me, in. Ben showed
them her ID and I was given a "Guest" tag by one of the men. One of
them ran his LED stick around both of us like he was making

silhouettes, then we were let in. His movement was so robotic, I held myself from touching his arm to feel whether he was actual flesh or metal. All the Ground Zero girls have IDs they wear like medals around their necks. They are to show it at the door to enter and to exit.

That morning, Ben and I drove to what looked to me like a modern but simple four-storey building with boutiques, coffee shop, a flower shop, basically, a commercial hub on Fola Osibo, in Lekki Phase 1. The ground floor of this building was one of the neatest carports I had ever seen, with white pillars demarcating the apportioned spaces for each car. I'm not sure if it is the adequate lighting or the fact that the walls were painted snow-white, but it looked extremely neat to me. There were also these heavy steal metal doors all over the carport and one of those doors (I swear I can never tell which one now) led us down a fleet of stairs .For some weird reason, the picture of Alice falling down the rabbit hole kept playing on my mind. We climbed one storey into the ground to this lavish space, where a TSA screener like the ones at airports is mounted. You drop your bags and belongings and then go through with no metals, just like at the airport. There was a sullen faced man sitting behind a glass, screening your stuff. He had a microphone that he talks into, to people passing through. I was so carried away looking at everything that I didn't realize there was anyone sitting there or that I had not dropped my phone and belt with the metal buckle along with my bag. I was promptly startled by a man's voice through a microphone. "Please drop your bag, phones and anything metal in the plastic trays and pass them through the screener. Thank you."

One thing that jumped out at me when we started down the "rabbit hole" was how cold this place was. I'm not sure what kind of ACs they installed down here, but it's like Antarctica compared to the humid Lagos weather. Back to my little tour. After you made it through the TSA screener, you get to the door with the two The-Thing-like men dressed military-style where the dancers and staff show their IDs to get in. Pass those two and you'll enter the most unique and luxurious lounge you'd ever set eyes on. I promise you, you have never seen anything like this. The rug beneath our feet felt like the softest sponge of ostrich feathers; it was like walking on cotton candy. This is what being a super-rich person must feel like. I didn't even think it was possible to have such a rug in ones' everyday life. It was so luxurious, my mind wouldn't accept it as a daily experience. It seemed to me like something one experienced once or never at all in a lifetime. The seats in the lounge were those recliners you find only in the first class section of an international flight, you know, the ones that can become a bed on demand. I remember the first and only time I flew first class back to Nigeria from London with Baba Agba. It was a British airways flight and I was about twelve years old. I often wish I could swipe that one golden opportunity and experience it as an adult. At twelve, I didn't fully utilize the experience like I would have now. I remember it was going to be Baba Agba's birthday in a week's time and he had visited London and was returning home. He had wanted all his children and grandchildren at his party, but Mummy Kay had an upcoming exam and could not come with us. The first class wing at Heathrow's Terminal 5 was very scanty that day. I think we were only three persons travelling first class; Baba Agba, an Indian man and me. From the private check-in to the luxurious suite on the flight, I felt like royalty. I'd never forget that experience because I tried sushi for the first time and my relationship with fish has been complicated ever since. Being a child and the only female in our wing, the male flight attendant doted on me so much that I felt like I could give him a hug and tell him my deepest secret. This of course, was way before I ever learnt of a corporate concept called customer service.

I was on a two-month probation at Ground Zero and I was to work twice a week, Tuesdays and Thursdays. The shows started at 10pm and we wound down at 4am. But before all of this began, I had to train for six straight months. By the second week, I was thinking I was a little way in over my head. My body shut down from all the stress at work, learning all that dance and choreography after work at Ground Zero and all the weekend lectures in psychology, etiquette and how to make people like me. Add that to the energy my relationship with Nomso was exuding and Caesar's need for his mummy and what you get equals a very skinny, miserable and sick Misi Okeke. I was suffering from exhaustion and I needed time away from my life to recuperate. I had made up my mind to quit Ground Zero and stop all the foolishness. What I hadn't realized was that it was August already and the Courts went on a lengthy vacation.

It had been a stressful but great year so far for Rhodes Legal. Our litigation department kicked off nicely and we had hired two more competent lawyers to join Adelomo and I. Oh, by the way, we won Ben's case against her Director. It eventually came down to an out-of-court settlement. Our percentage was a huge sum and my law firm gave me a fat bonus. Ben got her money and a public apology from Mr. Director in a major newspaper for full seven days. That should teach him a lesson. With the Courts on recess, I had enough time on my hands away from work to focus on my new job.

The space called Ground Zero was larger than I had seen on the day of my interview. There was a large conference room where we had lectures every Saturday and Sunday. Our lectures included psychology, etiquette and likeability, all aimed at how to influence people and make them like you. This was no joke. A professor of Psychology who was simply addressed as "Professor", taught us. There was a comprehensive lesson on shame and why shame is a programmed emotion and why we needed to let go of it. Gosh! It was all so psychedelic, like being a Nazi. Nuances of perversion spoken to you ever so lightly and gently, maybe even academically, until they begin to sip through your pores and attach themselves at your very core without you even noticing. It made me think of my interview with Uncle on my first day. It was the weirdest thing in the history of far-outs. I recall walking into Uncle's office for my interview and for a second, I thought I was standing in this room with glass walls looking out over some blue mass of water, like a belvedere. Then I remembered we were more than six feet under Lagos soil. The wallpaper was mind-falteringly good. I'm standing before "Notorious BIG", waiting for my interview to start and he is looking back into my eyeballs like he is waiting for me to start my own interview. I had never felt so exposed. I nervously said, "Good morning Sir, my name is Misi and I'm here for my interview." Radio silence. He continued looking at me intensely like a deaf architect studying an excavation site. After what seemed like forever, he said "Tell me about one traumatic experience in your past." I wasn't sure I heard him correctly. "Sir, I'm not sure I got that." I stuttered. He looked on for another 10 seconds before saying "I'd like to hear about one tragic event in your past." I thought explaining Adewale Briggs' absenteeism in my life may be too long and too intricate, maybe even boring so I just blurted out, "I was sexually molested by some..." I wanted to say father-figure, but that word 'father' had no place next to Timothée Moreau, so I said "...somebody I trusted once." Surprisingly, Uncle was nodding his head slowly like he had finally understood algebra after a long slow era of ignorance. He kept looking at me and then finally said "How did that make you feel?" I said "Pissed off!" and he continued his strange inappropriate nod. He said the strangest thing next "In here is the place to dance off that anger. I'll call you Yuki." I said "Sir, what's that?" "It's Japanese for happiness." He replied. "You look like you could use some of that. Wait outside, would you?" That was the end of my bizarre interview. After about forty minutes, his secretary handed me a work tag with YUKI written across the front, a list of the dance classes and courses, with the attendance schedule. I was to start my training in the coming week. The dance teacher/trainer, Chat (pronounced *sha*), an American professional dance, pole and aerial trainer, acclaimed to have performed a few times at the Cirque du soleil stage, was coming in to meet and train me in dance. As if the whole Notorious BIG Ground Zero experience wasn't intimidating enough. I wanted to drop my YUKI tag and run as far away as ever! What had I gotten myself into? Ben saw the fear imprinted on my face and started laughing. "Misi, ma je k'eruba e. "She said in her usual playful manner, hugging me. "Chat is very nice and patient and I think you'll love her." She added.

That night, after I had put Caesar to bed and Nomso was out late with God knows who, I thought about what Uncle, a complete stranger had said to me about happiness. "You look like you could use some of that." How dare he! I thought defensively. Just because I came to that stupid little club for an interview doesn't give him the right to appropriate virtues or a name to me. I was told the other girls picked their names based on the stage persona they wanted to portray, "So what made this ogbeni think that he could just throw a name at me? And on top of that sef, tell me whether I was happy or not?" But somewhere at the back of my mind, I knew that Uncle was right and the fact that he, a stranger could see that from the first few mostly-silent minutes of our meeting scared me the most. I had been carrying on, going about my duties almost *zoombieshly*, trying not to feel the emptiness or aloneness that had now wrapped itself like protective feathers around me. It was almost like Nomso and I were on an avoid-each-other mission these days and for the first time in the longest time, I just felt absolutely alone. Well actually, lonely, but I hate that word so I'd go with alone. As an only child of my parents, I grew up always engaged in something. I'm not sure if it was a conscious thing or it was simply my aunty, Mummy Kay, who made sure she gainfully utilized my time and mind. I was in dance class (ballet precisely) and book clubs throughout my primary and secondary education. I wrote essays for our school magazine and recited "Invictus" at my graduation from primary school. I was always doing something useful or as an older child, hanging out with my older men. I didn't know what the feeling of loneliness was like. I think I feared ever feeling it because it always seemed looming, not too far from me, resolute and a permanent dark shadow, hovering just a few yards away from my almost sunny life.

In the weeks and months that followed, I worked hard at Rhodes, trained harder at Ground Zero and Ben and I started to create a persona for Yuki. She was happiness after all, so she was going to make all of her spectators very happy and she was going to do it wearing white. We were allowed to design our costumes and that's exactly what I did. Ground Zero had a costume maker who was known as *Magic* on the premises. This lady made to the 'T' whatever designs the girls came up with. Alternatively, we had the choice of picking what we wanted to wear from a room full of color and the wildest racks of costumes you have ever seen. All kinds of wigs in all kinds of cuts and colors. This room was a fairy tale and I always feel like a child in a candy bowl when I am in it.

When I thought of Yuki's persona I thought of snow. Soft but cold, light but icy and just when you thought you'd gotten it, it melts away. She made her spectators happy but it was glazed. I fell in love with her fleeting nature because in some way, I was like that too. Her costumes where always mostly white, because I wanted her to stand out. Her masquerade masks were elaborate with white feathers, sequin, lace or beads. It made it impossible to see the girl behind the show and that was exactly what I was aiming for. I couldn't risk anybody in Misi's life finding out or even suspecting that she knew or was Yuki. Ben's persona was a blend of Cat Woman and Moulin Rouge. She's always liked the feline *bad-assness* so we found a way to fuse Cat Woman and the cabaret. Unlike Yuki, Ben's signature color was black. According to her, Yohji Yamamoto once said black is modest and arrogant at the same time and she wanted to capture the essence of that in her persona. So it was always black; black leather, black lace, black belts, black straps, black sequin.

As with everything in my life, Yuki went at this dance thing with everything. She practiced hard and had Chat on speed dial. They talked about the moves as well as practiced them at Ground Zero. They started from a basic split to other beginner's pole moves like scissor sit, pole sit, pirouette, knee bridge, hook and roll and speed bump. Yuki danced mostly in beginner's moves but I wanted her to always close with an advanced move like a jade split, to wow her guests. With lap dance, Chat taught Yuki that it was 90% about intimacy, feeling sexy and connecting with your spectator and 10% about dancing. I made Yuki always cajole up the image of an ex I had great chemistry with and made her imagine she was giving him the lap dance of his life.

It was a rainy Tuesday night in October the first time Yuki danced on the Ground Zero stage. It was such a nostalgic out-of-body experience. For her first dance, she cajoled up the ghosts of Tolu Makinwa and imagined he was every man sitting in the gallery. She imagined he had reappeared and was begging to come back into her life and she, interested but hesitant, decided to show him what he had missed all these years. I think Yuki danced her tail feathers off literally. Her costume that night was like the queen of the carnival; silver beaded panties and bra, an elaborate but light head gear dripping with feathers and crystal beads with a sequined eye mask. The gear was strapped so securely to her head that it became an extension of it. You would have had to behead her to get that head gear off Yuki.

Every girl's first dance was made special at Ground Zero. Whether you nailed it or goofed it on the first day, you really didn't know. If you noticed a lot of men watching you dance in the gallery you probably know that you were doing something right. But then again, bad press gets you bigger publicity doesn't it? The lounge announced your name and said you were dancing for the first time on the Ground Zero stage right before your grand entrance. Management left a bouquet of flowers, a bottle of expensive champagne and a you-are-doing-just-fine note on your dressing table, so that after your first "grind", you came back to feeling seen, maybe even loved. It was mind altering to say the least, that Ground Zero's sinister management understood that most of us dancing girls, as any girls in the world, had cravings that were so straight forward, honest and universal. We just wanted to be loved. How could any girl not give this place their best?

Chat always stayed for our first dance. She wore her signature poker face so you never knew what she was thinking. She would take mental notes of areas she needed to work on with you but she never criticized, only encouraged. From her reaction that night, I know Yuki killed it! I left Ground Zero at 4am the next day and was to be in court before 9am that morning. Everything worked against me that Tuesday. It was like the universe had conspired to stop me from my first day at the lounge and it took nothing but sheer rebellion to make it to the stage that night. First of all, court was irretrievably packed that Tuesday. The cause list that day was as long as time and we were at the tail end of the list. Adelomo and I left court at about 4pm. It was raining violently by the time I got home. I thought I would sleep a bit before the show, but no! Caesar had a bad fever and wouldn't stop crying. Whereas, Nomso was nowhere around. These days he left no messages about his whereabouts and quite frankly, I didn't care. I took Caesar to our estate's clinic, which I had never been to before. But considering that I had to be on stage for the first time at 10:40pm, I couldn't risk getting into the traffic and the rain to the hospital. Turns out it was an ear infection. By the time we got home, it was about 9:20pm. I had a quick bath, left an-I'm-off-to-my-second-job-so-that-we-can-be-comfortable note for Nomso. Thank God for Miss Jane, my not-so-new but competent nanny.

By the time I got to Ground Zero, it was 10:30pm. I had 10 minutes to change and then I heard them announce: "Dancing for the first time on the Ground Zero stage, please welcome, Yuki."

CHAPTER TEN
ALONE

***

*T*he day I told Nomso that I got another job to support us was as usual a day in the Okeke household as every other one - silent, tensed and saturated atmosphere, save for Caesar's babblings and occasional cries, laughs or shouts. My new job announcement bounced around the room and came back to me unnoticed and untouched. If Nomso heard me, he made neither sound nor move to show that he did. He finished his breakfast in a deafening high pitch silence, stroked Caesar's shaggy hair then proceeded to the study. "Nomso! Did you hear a word I said?" I was following him now with chest-expanding breaths like an inexperienced runner. "Yemisi, do whatever you like. You always have, just leave me out of it." came his lazy reply. He always called me Yemisi when all was not well between us and I was getting used to that these days. On happier days, which now seem like in another life, I was Misi. "So this is the thanks I get right?! Nomso, this is what I get for carrying this family, for doing my responsibility and yours? Right? " "You know what Yemisi, nobody asked you to *"carry"* this family." He made the quote-unquote sign in the air with both hands with the deadest sarcastic look on his face. He just looked absolutely devoid of any affection for me. "Or do my responsibility. Clearly you want to be a man so go be one!" He yelled, eyes bulging. "I may not be working at the moment, but I make sure that the rent is paid, Caesar's school fees is paid, so I don't know what you are talking about." He added with his back to me. "No Nomso. You don't make sure, your mum makes sure and I'm sick of the handouts! When are you going to stand up on your own? At least I'm trying. I really can't say the same for you." I said finding his face. "Work ten jobs if you like Yemisi Briggs, I do not care!" He said slamming his laptop and leaving me by myself as usual. Being one who never ever backed down from a fight, I yelled back running after him now, "Oh! So you're going to toss me back to my family now? I am now all of a sudden Briggs abi? Who even wants to be Okeke sef!" If that last part was my attempt to get a reaction from Nomso, it was clearly a futile one because he was in his car by now, revving out of the compound. This, like I said was a usual day at the Okeke residence and it always ended with me being alone.

CHAPTER ELEVEN

THE WEIGHT OF NO-GUILT

***

*C*an I just tell you how alive Misi feels since Yuki started shaking her tail feathers on Ground Zero stage? It's the most powerful feeling in the world. I'm not even sure the grand plan was for humans to feel alive all the time. It would be too much. There is a reason why we have to "find" what makes us feel alive. Some people leave this world without ever finding it. I think if we all found what made us feel alive, we will be too powerful.

Misi would walk into a court room and the presiding judge would be one of Yuki's drooling spectators or a man she gave a good lap dance to from a few nights before. The best part was, these men were unsuspecting of Misi. Omg! This is how God must feel, all-knowing of our dirty little secrets. It was like she was playing voyeur in the lives of the mightiest of mighty in this country. All kinds of men, dancing only feet's away from them, touching their fantasies, stroking their wildest, dirtiest thoughts, teasing their primal needs and sometimes lap dancing over their shameless erect groins. Misi has always been intimidated by the calibre of men that sit in that gallery every night, wanting to be entertained. But Yuki? Yuki is the most fearless bitch on God's rotating earth. Once she gets on that stage, it's like something takes over. She is calm, deliberate and executing to the last detail. Always smiling a playful sensual smile. Men do not throw money at the girls like they do in strip clubs. There are a non-stop stream of girls making the rounds in stripper heels, the tiniest and tightest of shorts and crop tops, taking orders and serving drinks, liquor, cigars, cigarettes on shiny trays. These trays also conveyed money in different currencies and phone numbers from the happy men to the dancing girl(s) of their liking. Any money passed to you while dancing was yours. The girls usually stuffed their 'loot' sensually in their costumes, inculcating it into their dance routines. Ground Zero considered it a complimentary gift to the girls for their "grind". Yuki had quite a number of good nights when she went home with $100 bills stashed deep in her wallet. Onetime, a man who had requested a private lap dance gave her N200,000 in crisp notes and his phone number. He kept sticking out his tongue like an expectant snake and whispering "Please call me." in Yuki's ear. She pushed him away in an improvised eleventh hour move with a forced laugh that must have seemed to him as part of the dance routine, whereas in actual fact, she just needed to stop him from oiling her ear with his slippery lengthy tongue.

One day, I was at the galleria at Lekki, spending Yuki's hard-earned Ground Zero money at a wig shop when I saw a very familiar figure along the corridor. It was Tolu. "Tolu Makinwa, as I live and breathe." I called out to him. He turned and walked into the wig shop. "No way! Yemisi Briggs, you still in Lagos?" He asked grabbing me up from the stool I was sitting in into a tight hug I was unprepared for. "How long has it been?" he asked leading me out to the corridor. "Forever!" I said. "How are you and what's good? You look the same by the way!" He was looking at me carefully now with a smile playing around his lips. "I'm married now with a kid" I said. "No! Misi, you? Married? And he's not me? Any chance the kid's mine and I don't know yet?" He said laughing wildly now. I realized how much I'd missed him. "No, the kid isn't yours I'm certain of that Tolu and yes, the hubby isn't you either." I replied. We stood out there talking for so long and then Tolu asked me to come back to his place for a meal. He had just moved in to a new apartment and was decorating and he needed my input he said. I was all so glad to go with him and somewhere at the back of my mind, I knew it had nothing to do with his decorating or new place and everything to do with the fact that we both had voids we were trying to fill.

There are very few people in the world today who can adhere uncompromisingly to a moral and ethical principle; I think that's what English language calls integrity. For example, holding another's secrets to heart and not ever telling. That's hard core. One of such persons, you know the few integrity people, if it was a person, would be the sofa in Tolu's living room. Here in Nigeria, most people refer to it as couch. That's the only furniture that made it from his old place to the new. A two and a half sitter chesterfield, upholstered in carton brown quilted leather, with a buttoned back. It simply has the ability to define the style of any space. Seeing it again at his new place made me think about a lot of things. Firstly, I always thought that sofa had such a presence about it, I mean if it was a guy, it'd probably be called Maximilian, or something *boujee* like that. I've always wondered about people who buy used sofas though. Again, I'm no superstitious girl, but sofas hold such secrets, such movements, stories, maybe even promises and of course, sweat and grim (eww). They sag over the years under all that weight.

Tolu's couch was a love nest, a war zone, a bed, a chair, an enemy of productivity, a solace giving friend and a reliable knee support when Tolu and I were at the doggy or any other..., a snuggle nest, everything.

For some people, love comes into their rooms, kicks her shoes off, finds the most comfortable sofa, lies down and rests, with no intention of going anywhere. For others, love walks in smoking a cigarette, checking her watch every two seconds, jittery, with one hand on the doorknob, heart rate up, always in sprinter's position, ready to run. Tolu reminds me of love in the latter form. Strangely, for someone who was so finicky about hygiene, he didn't have Maximillian cleaned out for the longest time. I remember when he told me back then when we were playing friends-with-benefits, that whenever he missed me, all he needed to do was lie or sit on his couch and he would get a nose full of my scent and he'd feel closer to me.

We tore at each other the second his front door closed behind us like wildings in heat season. It was almost like time had not passed between us.

I think that was the best sex I have ever had and if Tolu wasn't so slippery he'd probably say the same thing too. I left his apartment late that evening feeling light and content but also innately sad. I am so many things but a cheat isn't on that list. I had never cheated on Nomso before now. The idea of it had never even crossed my mind, but I had just performed adultery with Tolu so skillfully and so guiltlessly that it scared me. I was in deep thought in the days that followed. Did I even like Nomso? If I did, wouldn't I have hesitated for at least a second when I was with Tolu? Did I even respect my vows? Why didn't I feel any guilt? Why did I feel like I deserved to be loved even if it wasn't by my spouse? No questions asked, no rules and by somebody that also wanted me. These days, it felt like Nomso didn't even like me. I missed Tolu and my time with him made me acutely aware of the things that were lacking in my relationship with Nomso. Talk, play, a connection, romance, touch, like, chemistry, love. Do these things just happen between two people or you have to deliberately build them?

I saw Tolu again a couple of times actually, at his apartment. I'd drop by there for a quick 'fix' after work before going home to prepare for my night job. It was hard. Adultery is hard. It's like chasing the clock physically and emotionally. Some days I'd drive to Tolu's after work, in traffic only to get there and he'd be in some weird mood or he'd say he had to leave for an impromptu work meeting. I'd get home frustrated and take it out on whoever was in my way. Week days became impossible so I'd see him on Saturdays or Sundays. Time I should have been spending with my son who hardly saw me during the week. One Saturday, I sneaked out of the house so Caesar wouldn't see me and insist on following me out. It was raining that morning, I drove to Tolu's place only to see another female there. I didn't even wait to talk to him. There was no need for words. I left quietly and never saw him again and in typical Tolu fashion, he didn't bother to find me out. It was bad enough that I had to go the adultery route to get any kind of attention from a man, but to have to get that damn attention by competition with other unworthy contestants (he always had the worst taste in women anyways, why am I not surprised?) was a sport I was very unwilling to play. Not at this age or time in my life. The sneaky lifestyle had never really been my thing anyway and I hated carrying the weight of a no-guilt around Lagos.

CHAPTER TWELVE
SUNK

***

The pay at Ground Zero was so good, I could have quit my daytime job and we would have been just fine financially. But I couldn't risk Nomso or anybody finding out what this night shift job was really about. Besides, he had told Bebe that I was ungrateful for her input in our lives at this time that he was struggling, such that I had taken up a night shift job just to prove to him that I didn't need his family's money. Bebe being the wise woman that she is, called my Mummy Kay to inform her of this development. The picture Nomso painted to his mum, which was in turn replicated to Mummy Kay, was that I had neglected my husband and child on a quest for more money because I was tired of handouts. Of course, Mummy kay called me immediately, "Oluwayemis iAbidemi Briggs Okeke, kíniẹlẹ́ yìitímò n gbó? What is this I am hearing?" You knew it was serious when she called your full name. "Ẹkúrọ`lẹ́ màámi." I greeted her, knowing what all the fuss was about and feeling tired about it.

"Káalẹ́." She replied impatiently. "Ṣé o fẹ́ pa ara ẹ Yemisi? Do you want to kill yourself? Ehn? Báwoni o se lèmáas'iṣẹ́mẹ̀jì? When I am still alive this girl! Ṣé ofẹ́ pa mí? Do you want to kill me?" On and on she went with her monologue that required no contributions from me. "Ìdánwòránpẹ́l'ọkọẹ n làkọjá. It's only a fleeting phase Yemisi, your husband is not going to be jobless forever. Músùú rùfun. Be patient with him please. Óyá, kíniiṣẹ́kejìtí ò n ṣe? What's the second job? In short, wò ó,Yemisi, miò fẹ́ mọ̀. I don't want to know. Just quit it. Ṣ'otigbó mi?Èminiìyáẹ, màádẹ̀pèsèohungbogbotí o nílò." She finally came up for air. "Bẹ́ẹ̀ni mà." I replied, making a rumpled face and kicking the air in rebellion. That was never going to happen though. I was too invested now and I had put in too much for Nomso to use his usual arsenal aka our mothers, against me. I realized that none of them even knew what this night shift job was. I decided to tell Nomso that I was diversifying my work experience by night shifting as a manager and attendant at a 24-hour pharmacy in Ikoyi. You already know how that conversation went. Anyway, I didn't quit my night job and I didn't know anybody that would have made me.

Life was good. It was so hard to stay humble and under the raider when I was now making so much. I splurged on spa dates, perfumes, weekend trips with Caesar and Ben to beautiful locations in and around Lagos. I had cut down my hours at Rhodes and negotiated a good percentage per case. Life was almost beautiful but then, there was Nomso. Try as I may, I just couldn't get it right with him. I tried to befriend him, but he stayed distant and cold. I planned a dinner date for two so that we could talk and try to work things out but he refused to go. He said the only thing that would make us go back to being good was if I quit my new job. He said I was trying to make him look bad, bla bla bla. It just seemed like a concluded bye-bye to our erstwhile friendship because I really was not going to quit Ground Zero and nobody was going to make me. Maybe if the act became stale and boring to me I may consider quitting, but not now when everything was new and so life-giving.

Women are becoming the men that they want to marry. Assured, self-reliant, economically independent, sexually liberal and hopefully, with a nice apartment. I think I speak for most women when I say that what we want in a good husband is kindness, respect, adventurousness, curiosity and a dynamo in the bedroom. A keeper basically.

Ben was leaving; it was the end of an era! She had saved up enough to start a new life in Canada. I couldn't shake the feeling of abandonment that had started clotting down the hollow of my guts when she announced her departure to me over lunch one fine day. I always reaffirmed to myself mostly out loud that I was fine and that people will come and go. But deep down inside, if you looked, you'd see the gangrene of abandonment spread endlessly like skin all over me. Who would blame me though, my history in a sense has been littered with rejection. I usually wouldn't admit it, not even to myself but this feeling is so total and acute that I feel abandoned even when Caesar's nannies leave.

CHAPTER THIRTEEN

AN ENCOUNTER

***

I'm a bag lady. I believe that a woman's handbag is an extension of herself. It's the only place where all the different parts of her life converge. Which is why looking inside other people's bags is so interesting. On the outside, a woman would tick all her boxes- hair, shoes, make-up, clothes, check, check, check. Inside her bag, you see her real self: an iphone, lipstick in a color she'd never wear to work, day after pills, a child's teddy, a pack of Durex, an emergency tooth brush, a card of paracetamol for stress headaches you'd never dream she has because she seems so able.

All a girl needs for a tip-top handbag collection is a good eye and a slightly impulsive nature. My best buy till date remains a black Celine nano belt bag in crocodile embossed calfskin, originally priced at £1600. Phew! When I was in the university, My Jamaican friend Tracey knew this rich old white lady that was doing a yard sale. She owned a big castle-like house out in Bristol. So we drove up there and it was love at first sight, me and the Celine. The lady priced it at £100. I begged and begged for a discount but she was adamant. In the end, the bag was equivalent to me getting fresh braids, so I consoled myself for spending that much in one afternoon. I don't carry it often in Nigeria because of the harsh weather and I had never seen any other person with that bag. In fact, I would brag to Gogo and Lola then that I owned the only Celine nano belt bag in all of Lagos (the only original piece that is), until one fine day, I saw a lady with the same bag but in brown.

I was at a super mart in Ikoyi buying groceries with Lola. It was one of those rare weekends when she was back in town and had called me to meet up. Her house was devoid of food and supplies due to her latest sojourn out of town. Lola was pushing the cart while I was getting stuff off the shelf when this tall slender woman walked past our isle, holding a little girl's hand in her right hand and her Celine purse in the left hand. Lola saw the purse first and almost shoved me down. "There's your competition." She said folding her arms with an "Uhun" look on her face. "What competition? What do you mean Lola?" I asked, a little confused. "The lady with the other Celine nano, live in Lagos!" She almost screamed. I turned just in time to see the lady walk past us with it. "Maybe it's a fake." I said, feigning disappointment. "It doesn't look fake to me." She insisted. "Lola, how would you know that from way over here." I said. "Let's follow her." She announced covertly, dragging me along and jetting off with the cart before I realized we were on a Celine nano bag-owner man hunt. "Why?!" I asked. Almost sliding off the sleek floors. "Because you've tormented us enough in this Lagos about that stupid purse." Lola said in motion.

It was the most ridiculous thing ever, but it was also so-Lola. Spontaneous and in the moment. In our short sprint towards my nano purse comrade, all I was thinking was will Lola grab the purse from the unsuspecting woman with the child and demand to check for its originality or what? Did she even have a plan? And why exactly were we running? The lady who had got something off the shelf was at one of the check-out stands by now, talking to a man. The little girl was grappling for the man's attention and instinctively I knew he was the tall lady's husband and the little girl's dad. The man was off-loading a cart at the check-out stand and he had his back to Lola and I. I stopped dead in my tracks as if I had seen a ghost. Even if I had blind folds on, I would recognize that back anywhere. That height that towers. He looked a little weightier but still in great shape. They, all three of them, looked like the perfect family and the tall slender woman looked happy and content. I couldn't help thinking this should've been my mum and the little girl should have been me because the man with the back to us was Adewale Briggs, my father.

I couldn't move. I tried to hide and just watch them like the peeping tom I had become; hiding behind masks and peeping into other peoples' privacies. But the shelves at the store couldn't hide me, neither were there any masks here to shield me from my own brutal privacy. He had died to me. Not that he had made much of a difference in my life alive though. But when he left London years ago to start his life in Nigeria, I considered myself an orphan. A lucky one, because I had my aunt who was more than two parents to me. I had never thought about him again and he had never contacted me. Not while I was still in the UK or even when I moved back to Nigeria. I know he and Mummy Kay were still cordial. "Misi, you ok? Do you know those people?" Lola was saying beside me but her voice seemed so far away. It seemed like I was in an anaesthetictrance, only this time I was wide awake. Just then the tall man looked down at the little girl and something seemed to catch his attention behind him. I raced to the nearest shelf but it was too late. "Yemisi, is that you?" I heard him say in his deep rich voice. If I were to pay him a compliment, he came carefully made. He was a very good looking man with an intimidating height and brown skin like me. His had a rich and deep tone, with a body built like an athlete's.

I was resolved not to leave that shelf. If he wanted to talk to me he was going to have to sweat it over. But even that was a more dangerous option. I shut my eyes tight like I was about to be given an injection. "Misi, what is going on here?" Lola said slapping my eyes open. "That man, that's Adewale Briggs." I whispered, shutting my eyes again for another "injection"."That's your dad?" Lola said bulgy eyed. Adewale walked over as I knew he would. He had a cool, calm, collected way about him and even now, I smelled his cologne. It was woody and intoxicating like I remember it. He had a concerned look on his face and before he could get to me Lola stepped in front of him, arms crossed in front of her, wearing her active bitch face. "She doesn't wish to speak to you Sir." Lola said to him, looking him straight in the pupil. She would've been looking up at him but for the heels she was wearing. Thank God for those heels! There was something eternally satisfying about measuring up face to face with the enemy when it came down to it. "Hello, young lady." I heard Adewale say to Lola. I was still *statued* by the shelf, eyes wide shut. "I assume you are Yemisi's friend. My name is Adewale Briggs, her Father. She's lucky to have a friend like you, young lady." Manipulative bastard! I thought. I wanted to shout "Stop calling her young lady!"But it seemed my mouth was sealed too. He sounded so confident you would think he was about to give Lola an award for the greatest valedictorian speech of all time. "Yemisi, how are you?" He was talking to me with Lola still in front of him. I remained rooted by the shelf and my eyes were determined to stay closed. "Your aunty told me you moved back to Nigeria. I'd like to talk to you some time if that's ok." He brought out a card from his pocket and Lola snatched it from him immediately so he wouldn't get any near me. "Take care now." He said and was gone. By now the tall lady and her child were waiting for him outside in their car. Lola followed him to make sure he was gone and then ran back to my refuge shelf. Tears were streaming uncontrollably from my sealed eyes forming a pool around my feet. She hugged me tight and we stood there for a while. No words, just the comfort of being understood without explanation and being defended without a reason overwhelmed me more than seeing Adewale Briggs again.

Lola led me carefully to the car like I was delicately spun cotton, then went back into the store and paid for our stuff. "The cheek of that man! Paying me a compliment in the middle of a storm. Who does he think he is?" Lola said more to the car than to me as we drove back to hers. "My dad!" I said quietly and we burst out into relief laughter. It was such a good laugh, it hurt. That's the thing about true friends, they are always together in spirit.

As I laid sleepless in my bed that night, I thought about Adewale Briggs and why he still had that kind of power over me. Lola had handed me the card she snatched from him and I had thrown it out the window. He hadn't even thought it proper to introduce me to his "family". What was it about me that made him work so hard to keep me a secret? Why did he show off that tall woman and her daughter while he kept me in the shadows of the shelves? Why didn't he pull me out from those shelves into the light? I had too many questions and no answers. Maybe this was my chance to ask him all the questions I needed to know all these years. Maybe I should have been more courageous and stepped up to him in that store. And what kind of woman was the tall slender woman anyway? Why didn't she come over and say hello even if it was just to size me up? Didn't she even want to know who her husband's daughter was? Was she even told that I was his daughter? Why did it even bother me suddenly to be recognized by anybody as his daughter? But really, who was the more courageous one amongst us two? Adewale Briggs had been a coward all his life, at least when it concerned me, he was. He hid behind Mummy Kay all those years and never lived up to his responsibility as a father to a little girl who never met her mum. I was a child, that's all I was. It wasn't my responsibility to take care of my father's insecurities or fears. It was his job. I was the courageous one. I had found a way to grow up without him. I remember what Prof. Allen, my therapist said to me once about fathers. He said a father is a girls' standard of how she would measure every man that she meets in her life. I hated to think that maybe my thing for nice smelling men may have come from Adewale Briggs. Professor Allen inferred that the men I got intimately involved with were all absent, older, great conversationists, confident....Omg! They were all Adewale Briggs in some way, weren't they? I wanted to stop my mind from thinking at this point. I couldn't handle the pain I was feeling and the worst thing is, I didn't trust my relationship with Nomso well enough to share this cloud with him.

There are all kinds of aloneness in the world today. There is an only child aloneness, there is the aloneness of being by oneself and there is a widow or widower's aloneness. The worst kind however, is the type one feels while being surrounded by people. It's the type of aloneness that a married man or woman may feel while being married, while their spouse is still alive and well. It even has a synonym: loneliness. Now you see why I hate that word.

CHAPTER FOURTEEN
A CERTAIN STRONGNESS
BY ADEWALE BRIGGS

***

I couldn't believe my eyes. She's a spitting image of Tai. If I'm being honest, I haven't been very fair to the girl. She was collateral damage. Has always been. I warned Taiwo but she always had to have her way.

Taiwo Ajayi, the feistiest woman to have ever lived. There was no other woman for me. She was the loveliest and the scariest woman in the world. We met because she made the first move. I could never have talked to a girl like her back then. She was way out of my league. It was Kolade's birthday and he had a house party. Taiwo and her twin Keyinde, the hottest girls in GRA then, were invited. I was staying at Kolade's house at the time because of the messy revelation at mine. "Hello handsome." She came up to me with a drink in one hand. "Why aren't you dancing?" She shouted over the music. I was sitting in a corner enjoying the music because I didn't have the courage to ask any of the girls for a dance. "Do you want a drink?" She asked and handed me hers before I could even answer. "Let's dance." She pulled me off my sit. This girl definitely didn't wait for any cues. She had her leg on the peddle. She threw her arms around my neck when the blues started playing on the radio and the lights in the room turned red. Kolade and I had changed some of the bulbs in their living room to red earlier in the day, specially for the blues. "I like you, stranger."She whispered in my ear. "My name is Tai. It's short for Taiwo. What's yours?" "Wale. It's short for Adewale." I said into her ear. She laughed a hearty laugh and threw her head back like she had a nose bleed. Taiwo was my first everything concerning the opposite sex. I soon travelled to Leeds on a scholarship and we somehow went our separate ways until I visited Nigeria again. We were grown-ups by now. Nothing was said but we carried on like time hadn't passed. I still remember her call one afternoon while I was studying at the library. She sounded very calm, almost quiet. I had never heard her so quiet. She always had something to say. 'I'm pregnant Wale and it's yours." I couldn't believe it. I always thought Taiwo was exposed enough to know how to take care of herself. She seemed so aware of everything and I began to question if the baby was even mine. I told her I wasn't ready to be a dad. When I asked her if she was sure the baby was mine, all hell was let loose. She yelled into the phone non-stop for probably what seemed to me like forever. I put the phone away from my ear so I have no idea what obscenities she was hurling at me in Yoruba interpreted in English. What I eventually got out of that conversation when she was done yelling was that she had told her dad already and there was only one option for her. Marriage. She refused to hear me out. She wasn't getting rid of the pregnancy and she wasn't going to be a single mum, she threatened.

In the following days, her father, Baba Agba called me. I expressed my concerns to him about the baby's paternity and I remember how still he suddenly sounded on the phone. I could tell he was livid. "Listen to me young man, Taiwo is my first born and I have no reason to doubt what she tells me because I raised them right. For your sake I will conduct a DNA test on the baby when the doctor says it's safe to do so. Listen to me carefully, if that baby is yours? You will come home and do right by her. None of my children will be baby factories for any man. Ṣ'ogbọ́?" He said in anger and went off the phone.

The baby turned out to be mine according to the DNA test they sent to my mail. I'm not sure if I believe the test to this day or my mind just wants to put Yemisi in the same position I was put in as regards paternity. It felt like they manipulated me into marriage. I wasn't ready for it. I knew I had personal issues to deal with and I needed therapy, but those early days in England, trying to get a Bachelors degree and trying to make a first class was no facile feat and I couldn't add a family to it. I simply wasn't emotionally prepared for it. I resented Taiwo for it all. She reminded me of Idowu Bolatito Briggs. People who manipulate situations and other people for their selfish needs. I travelled home for the marriage ceremonies but returned back to UK almost immediately because I had enrolled for a Masters degree. I think I did that to keep away from the treachery I had at home as a wife. Maybe Yemisi and I would have had a chance if I wasn't cajoled to marry her mum. I just didn't know what to do with a wife and child then.

Years after I had been to therapy and done the work, I felt like I was getting married on my own terms to a woman I really knew and loved. With Taiwo, it just seemed like I was submerged. She sort of commandeered everything between us and I felt like I didn't even know myself well enough to know if I really liked her or not. She was so larger than life. Her twin, Keyinde, was easier to talk to and less volcanic. Sadly, Yemisi was caught in the middle of all of this mess but I just didn't have anything to offer her. When Keyinde offered to raise her after Taiwo's unfortunate demise, I felt like I had been given a second chance. But she just reminded me of her mother and her paternal grandmother's manipulation. I'm a different person now, thanks to therapy and the love and support of Bunmi my wife and our daughter, Ife. I would like to have a cordial relationship with Yemisi someday, but it seems like it's too late. She has a certain strongness about her that is so Taiwo Ajayi Briggs. A strongness that scares me and that I resent so much.

CHAPTER FIFTEEN
PANDORA

***

Nomso is a model employee. He is the dude that takes home all the best-staff awards at work. When he was at the bank, he was a sterling staff and he built great customer-client relationships so much that a lot of these "rich kids" befriended him. One of such kids is Lekan Babatunde, a Risk Management Specialist at Microsoft, UK. Lekan met Nomso at the bank the day he went with his mum to sort out her bank troubles. They found out that Lekan's mother and Nomso's mother were very good friends .Nomso was invited over to the Babatunde's mansion for lunch and every other special occasion thereafter. The two guys fast became friends. All of these happened way before Nomso and I ever crossed paths and although Lekan returned to the UK and was married now with kids, they managed to stay in touch. I had never met Lekan but had my ears full about him back then when the going was good with Nomso and I.

It was a Tuesday night. I didn't go to Rhodes that day. I wrote a brief at home, spent time with Caesar after school and just relaxed in anticipation of the show I had that night. Nomso had been out all day as usual and there was no telling when he would get back. I had a bath, dressed up, kissed a reluctant Caesar goodnight and drove to Ground Zero. My dance was at 11:30pm and the gallery seemed packed that night. A group of excited young men walked in while I was dancing and shortly after, the DJ announced that it was somebody's birthday. From the noise and activity around the little group, it seemed like it was one of the guys. Usually, when it was somebody's birthday and they choose to announce it at Ground Zero, it automatically earned them a lap dance from the girl performing on the stage. These young men with the energy of boys had settled in the reclining chairs turned beds and a spotlight was now on the birthday boy who was looking eager and a little nervous. The other guys were cheering, hooting and whistling as Yuki made her way slowly down the stage towards the spotlight where the birthday boy lay on his recliner. Yuki suddenly unceremoniously walked a fierce catwalk straight to him and did a full split across his legs, raised his chin up with her thumb and fore finger, looked him straight in the eye and whispered, "Happy birthday baby, how can I make you happy?" The other guys were ecstatic by now and the birthday boy had his hand shaped like an "O" over his mouth and releasing his laugh in bouts like a bad cough. Yuki was basking in the attention of this euphoria with her back now to the birthday boy when suddenly, her face mask was torn off her face by somebody who was now standing by the birthday boy. "Yemisi! Wait, wait. Yemisi!" came Nomso's voice. "Nomso mehn! What the fuck? Why would you jump in my grind like that?" The birthday boy said, standing up from his recliner. There was a commotion now and "The-Thing-like men" appeared from nowhere. "She's my fucking wife! Lekan, that's my fucking wife!" was all I could hear Nomso shouting as "The-Thing-like men carried him out of the lounge. "Yemisi! We are done! Fucking bitch! You've been lying right under my nose! Zara has always been right about you, you whore! Yemisi!" And his voice faded out as the little group disappeared after him.

In all our three-going-on-four years of marriage, I had never heard Nomso cuss. I couldn't move. I think I shared a kinship with Lot's wife in that moment. Numb to feelings, numb to touch, just a pillar of white salt, in my case white sequin and beads.One of the dancers, Ruby Woo, came and led me out to my dressing room. I leaned my weight on her like I was an earthquake victim being tugged from the wreckage. I just sat at my dresser staring into nothingness, until Uncle called me into his office. He gave me a week off to go sort my "house issues". I had never been more embarrassed.

The doors where securely locked to me when I got home that night. Nomso's phone was switched off and he must have commanded Miss Jane to switch off hers. I knocked, begged, I couldn't cry but I tried to. My efforts to get into the house were as useless as a single shoe. I eventually checked into the estate's guest house at 4am, the same time I should have been coming home from Ground Zero on a normal day. I was too tired but I didn't sleep a wink. I tried Nomso's phone all night. I sent him a thousand texts and I was at the house by 6am. The sight that greeted me were my things outside the front door in a messy pile. This time, I broke down in, I'm sure, the ugliest cry of my life. I couldn't stop. I had everything and I just threw it all away all on a quest to feel alive. Maybe we humans were made to stay mundane because it seems like most things that bring us to life are risky and dangerous. Like a bungee jump, or a steamy affair, or in my case, a double-faced wife and mother.

It's been a week since the incidence. I've been staying at Lola's place. Nomso hasn't said a word to me and I haven't seen Caesar since I kissed him goodnight that Tuesday night. In hindsight, I wish I called in sick that night and stayed home with Caesar. I would give everything up just to have my baby and not being able to see him or talk to him feels like lead on my heart. Mummy Kay has been calling me now for days but I'm not sure I'm ready to talk to her just yet. I thought about going back home to London but I am too ashamed to face her. What will I tell her? That I needed to strip because Nomso and I were in a bad place? Or that my life was such a routinely scripted corpse I needed to shock it back to life and save it from eternal banality. Would anybody understand my position? In some weird way, I enjoyed the attention those sordid strangers at the Ground Zero gallery gave me. They made me feel wanted and desired and sexy. All the things I needed but couldn't create in my relationship with Nomso. I could just picture in my mind's eye the Nigerian courts pronouncing me an unfit mother and granting full custody to Nomso. I saw Nomso, smoldering, silent in righteous indignity, the court of public opinion, blogs, social media tearing at me piece by piece like a vultures' banquet.

I took a week off work after the incidence. Whether by my choices or not, life had dealt me an unfair blow and I was about to lose everything I ever cared about. I couldn't re-enter the world too soon, I'd regret it. Like a wounded animal, I laid down on Lola's sofa in the living room in my sleeping robe and grieved. I wasn't sure of the day or the time as day became night and vice versa. It was a good time because Lola was out of town, therefore, there was nobody playing the voice of reason around me, 'cos the heavens know I didn't need that at this time.' I had comfort food which consisted mostly of junk: a bag of salty onion chips, biscuits, chocolates, sweets and a big bottle of whiskey (for shock). I never left that sofa all week, safe for my pee breaks. I re-watched 94 episodes, 6 seasons of Sex and the City and cried.

Gradually, through the gloom and Carrie Bradshaw's fashion, I was able to gather myself (or what was left of me) up from that sofa, have a long hot bath on the fifth day or so and I eventually re-engaged with the world again. I went back to work full time. I needed to get my mind off going crazy. A bailiff served me with a divorce petition from Nomso the other day and I quickly went straight to the page that listed the reason(s) for the request for dissolution of marriage. He listed my continuous refusal to perform my conjugal duties, adultery and that I was an unfit mother to our child and therefore that full custody of Caesar should be given to him. I was so grateful to him in that moment for not telling the world about the real reason we were divorcing. I went to my bosses, the partners at Rhodes and requested a closed-door meeting. They obliged me and I disclosed to them regrettably that I had a short-lived affair with somebody and my husband found out and was now requesting a divorce. I apologized for the embarrassment this petition may cast on the firm. One of the partners, Abosede Rhodes, volunteered to handle the case herself and discreetly too. I told them I did not want to contest the petition but they insisted we fight for custody of the child. Nomso knew I wouldn't dare fight over Caesar with him; not after he had done me a favour and concealed my dirty linens from the world. I knew he didn't have any proof of my time at ground zero and everything he said would amount to hear-say in court. I told Abosede Rhodes that I needed some time to try and work out the terms of custody with Nomso outside of the courtroom. If he continued being stubborn and insisting that I never see Caesar again then Rhodes will give it everything to get joint custody. My life was my son, and my son was my life and nobody, not even a hurt Nomso was going to take him away from me. Nomso's parents called Mummy Kay who flew in almost immediately. They are talking about us returning the bride price but my uncles and Mummy Kay want to try reconciliation. Nomso is adamant and unshakable in his resolve to never speak to me again or allow Caesar anywhere near me. Everything is happening so fast and everything seems so blurry and too heavy for me but I have no choice but to stay strong. Mummy Kay and I eventually talked about everything when she came home. "Yemisi, kilon sile`?"was all she asked me and I broke down.

There is something to be said about a person that knows when a hug is worth more than a thousand spoken words. My mother's twin is such a person. Keyinde Ajayi is a woman I will choose in a thousand lifetimes to be my mother. She just held me and cried with me until I stopped and could talk. "Màámi, I felt like I needed it. Mo ròpémonílátijẹ́ẹlòmíràn. You know, to survive the marriage." That was all I could say through my tears. She held my face with both her hands and looked at me squarely with tears streaming down her own face, "You took things too far, Yemisi. Mi ònípurọ́fún e, ọmọ mi.Óyẹkotiwás'ílé. You should have taken my grandson and come home for a while. I know, Yemisi, you were not in love with that boy, but for Babatunde's sake, you married him and that is the sacrifice a mother makes for her children. I know! Óyẹkotiwás'ílé. I know! Not every woman can go weak in the knees for a dependent man Yemisi. I understand." Mummy Kay said quietly, looking at the floor at something that seemed more inward than external. I was shocked to hear this and looked at her this time. "Yemisi." she continued, still looking at the innate object, "Ajayi women have been known only to fall for independent, alpha males. Your mother, myself, our mother, your great grandmother. It is evident in the kind of husbands they married. I understand you, omo mi, but you should have come home. Instead of taking matters into your hands. Ó dáa. Àtúnṣewà".

Mummy Kay and my uncles have swung into action with the in-laws to see if the matter can be resolved. She especially has been trying to get Nomso to let me see Caesar. I don't deserve her.

Abosede Rhodes has filed an answer to Nomso's petition and a counter Petition asking for joint custody of Caesar.

I have come to the cross road of my life. I am not a religious or superstitious girl, but there is something very otherworldly about a place where two roads meet. The devil is said to set up shop there for those who want to swap their souls for something more useful.

And if you believe that God can be bribed, it is also the hallowed ground to make sacrifices. Cross roads are the place to change direction, only in my case, I am not even the driver for the direction my life is about to take at this crossroad.

THE END

Printed in Great Britain
by Amazon

17281366R00075